REPROOF POSITIVE

Indignantly, Maarswell reprove her for ore the streets after darkou take risks you have no

"What risks?" Mary countered.

In answer, Captain Carswell pulled Mary to him and ruthlessly kissed her. It seemed to Mary that his lips meant to punish her, while his hands roamed familiarly over her body.

"That is a taste of what you would endure if you were unmasked by a gentleman of the town," he said grimly.

With bravado Mary replied, "And is that, then, the much vaunted passion between the sexes?"

"No," said Carswell. "This is." And his lips came down on hers again. . . .

CAPTAIN ROGUE
APRIL KIHLSTROM

A SIGNET BOOK

NEW AMERICAN LIBRARY

SIGNET, SIGNET CLASSIC, MENTOR, ONYX, PLUME,
MERIDIAN and NAL BOOKS are published by NAL
PENGUIN INC., 1633 Broadway, New York, New York 10019

First Printing, February, 1988

1 2 3 4 5 6 7 8 9

PRINTED IN THE UNITED STATES OF AMERICA

1

AS the public coach rumbled to a halt at the crossroads Captain Randall Carswell sighed in exasperation. He had been traveling some time already and was tired. Even his clothes, a brown jacket over tan pantaloons and a simple shirt beneath it all, had begun to rumple with the jolting ride. What, he wondered, was the problem this time?

To Captain Carswell's surprise and the grumblings of some of the other passengers, the driver opened the door of the coach and informed everyone that a young female person was about to join their company. Still, room was made for the newcomer and the driver good-naturedly promised to make up the lost time if they would just give him a chance and not delay him with their complaints. Captain Carswell doubted that was possible but, he acknowledged with an inward shrug, since he was traveling at a whim anyway, it really didn't matter how long the journey took. There was no one to expect him, no business to contract, no urgency to his travels. By contrast, the solicitor next to him was most distressed.

"If I am late," the poor fellow was trying to tell anyone who would listen, "Lord Gilly will be most annoyed, most annoyed indeed. I solemnly promised to call upon him by this evening at the latest. You, miss, did you think of that when you flagged down the carriage?"

The newcomer, startled at being so addressed, nevertheless managed to look amused as she replied, "No. How could I, sir? I had no notion of your existence, much less your troubles. I was, I confess, rather preoccupied with my own."

"Which were, no doubt, of the direst importance," Carswell found himself suggesting amiably.

The sparkle in the newcomer's eyes markedly deepened as she said, "But of course, sir. Do we not all think that about ourselves?"

Carswell laughed even as the solicitor snorted in disgust. "That is frank, at all events," the captain said. "Miss . . . ?"

The young woman hesitated perceptibly before she answered. "Miss Moira Fane. And your name, sir?"

"Nicholas. Nicholas Warford," the solicitor replied. "And I am on urgent business for the youngest son of the Duke of Winthrop, who is staying at one of his minor country houses, and he shan't appreciate this delay at all."

Only by the slightest twitching of her lips did Miss Fane betray her amusement. Equally discreet, Carswell merely said quietly, "And I am Captain Randall Carswell, late of the Hussar's division. Are you going far?"

"To Ipswich," Miss Fane replied. "I've some, er, business there."

"Business?" Warford protested. "Young

persons do not conduct business. Their employers conduct it for them."

It was clear to Captain Carswell that Warford had not thought to look beyond Miss Fane's drab cloak and country-girl dress of some cheap woollen material in judging her. He, however, had formed a rather different opinion of Miss Fane's circumstances. In a quiet voice he said, "I collect Miss Fane to mean her business in Ipswich is something in the nature of visiting relatives, perhaps?"

Miss Fane shook her head. "No," she said coolly, "I meant something rather in the nature of seeking a position to support myself. Finding a job, if you like to put it that way. I have reason to believe I may have a chance in Ipswich."

"Of course," Warford said in a speaking voice. "Though one might be forgiven for thinking your chances would be far better closer to your own home where you might have relatives and acquaintances to speak for you."

Once more Carswell came to her rescue. "Housemaid?" he hazarded innocently. "If so I must confess I agree that the gentry generally hire young women from families they know. Unless, of course, you mean to try with a merchant family. They might be a trifle less particular."

Miss Fane squared her shoulders. "No," she said with creditable calm. "I am going to Ipswich to be an actress. There is a theater there, you may know. Though if I did seek a domestic position it would be as a governess."

Both Warford and Carswell, it seemed, were caught with a fit of coughing at precisely the same time.

Warford recovered first. "This is worse than all

the rest," he said, his lips pursed in disapproval. "Evidently you are runaway from home and someone ought to fetch you back straightaway. As for acting, pah! Or governess. In the event you did not already know it, I take leave to inform you that governesses generally come of good families and are ladies themselves."

Stung, Miss Fane replied, "Well, and so I am a lady."

"Indeed!" Warford snorted. "You may as well try and tell me you are a member of the royal family! However you may have come by your admittedly genteel habits of speech, your clothing must betray you. No doubt this is more of your acting nonsense, but I tell you, girl, unless your feet are already irretrievably set upon the path of utter ruin you had best go home. Work for a few years in a genteel home, then settle down. Marry. Raise a family. That is the advice I give you."

Miss Fane looked to Carswell for assistance but, she noted bitterly, his shoulders were quivering with suppressed laughter. Nevertheless, he tried to come to her aid. "I do believe, Miss Fane," he said with mock gravity, "that you have shocked poor Mr. Warford."

This did not molify the solicitor in the least. "Soldiers! You are as bad as anyone," he said with the same distaste he had just shown Miss Fane. Then, to himself, he added, "I knew I should have hired a chaise and four. Lord Gilly would have stood the expense, if only to be sure I would arrive quite speedily. And then I need not have rubbed shoulders with such riffraff. I wonder, captain, that even you do not dislike it."

Carswell, however, as has been said, had already formed his own opinion of Miss Fane and it was not that she was either a farmer's daughter or future haymarket wares. Not, at any rate, if he could prevent it. For the first time since his discharge, the captain felt a strong stirring of interest in the events directly ahead of him. And when Miss Fane next regarded him he smiled with sufficient kindness at her that she was moved to ask, "And what is your destination, Captain Carswell?"

"Ipswich," he replied unhesitatingly.

"But you told me it was Lowestoft," the solicitor protested. "That's what you said not five minutes before the coach stopped for this young person." He paused and fixed Carswell with a disapproving stare. In a scathing voice he said, "I must hope this does not mean what I fear it means."

"And what is that?" Carswell asked politely.

"That you mean to encourage this young person on her path to ruin," Warford answered angrily.

Carswell flicked a speck of dust off the sleeve of his jacket. When he spoke it was with a coldness that froze his listeners. "I shall forgive you for that, Warford. Once. I should not, however, make the same mistake twice, if I were you." He paused and let the full measure of his stare have its effect upon the poor solicitor, who seemed positively to shrink before it. Then Carswell went on, "I should like to remind you that my route is not, cannot be, of any concern to someone such as yourself. And you flatter yourself if you believe you are privy to my thoughts. Miss Fane is in no danger from me, I assure you. Indeed, you flatter her too much when you suggest that I have altered my plans because of Miss Fane. I doubt she is so foolish as to make such a mistake."

Carswell turned to meet Miss Fane's eyes and

she choked slightly as she replied, as carelessly as she was able, "Of—of course not. That would be absurd."

"Good," Carswell told her frostily. Then he turned back to the solicitor. "Are you satisfied, pray tell, Mr. Warford?"

The poor fellow seemed to wilt completely under this Turkish treatment and he managed only a weak, "Absolutely," in reply. Nor was he above mopping his forehead in relief when Carswell turned his gaze away and became, apparently, lost in contemplation of the roof of the traveling coach.

When Warford finally quitted the stage at the point nearest Lord Gilly's estate, Carswell contented himself with saying that if Mr. Warford's powers of observation did not improve he was unlikely to distinguish himself in any career. Miss Fane hastily looked away and merely asked how far they were from Ipswich.

"Do you really mean to join the theater there?" Carswell asked, an amused smile upon his face.

"Why not?" Miss Fane asked stiffly.

Carswell chose his words carefully. "Well, do you know, I have the most absurd notion that your family would not be entirely pleased if they knew of your intentions."

Bitterness tinged Miss Fane's voice as she replied, "There is rent money needed for a room, food to be bought, clothes to wear, oh a thousand things to living, and they must be paid for somehow. And as I have no other talents, save for acting, what other choice is open to me?"

"Are you then entirely alone in the world?" Carswell asked with a frown. "No relatives at all?" He paused as a thought occurred to him, "Or is it that you have none on the, er, same side of the blanket?"

Miss Fane had schooled herself in anticipation of a great many questions, but this had not been one of them. Later she greatly regretted the relieved outburst of laughter that then prevented her from adopting what might have been a most useful story.

When she had recovered herself, Miss Fane avoid Carswell's eyes and answered resolutely, "I feel myself to have no alternative to the course of action I had undertaken."

Instead of the sympathetic reply she expected, however, Carswell said dryly, "That you feel this way does not, you must know, make it true."

"I no longer care to discuss the matter," Miss Fane retorted frostily. "You can have no knowledge of my circumstances."

"That is precisely the problem I am trying to rectify," Carswell pointed out innocently.

"Well, I do not intend to tell you anything further," Miss Fane replied with a distinct toss of her head and a sniff.

The other occupants of the coach who had been watching the exchange with something akin to delight now added their ideas.

"That's the ticket, miss."

"No business of 'is, your business."

"What are 'is circumstances?"

"Aye, cap'n. You tell 'er 'oo you are, first!"

Carswell looked about him, a smile twitching at the corners of his mouth. "Very well," he said amiably. "*I've* nothing to hide. I have just come from the Continent. Sold out my colors at the insistence of my superior officer." He paused, seeming almost to enjoy the looks of shock and anger that were directed at him. When satisfied he went on, without haste, "For medical reasons, of course. An, er, unfortunate wound that while it does not entirely incapacitate me, does render me less than useful as a soldier."

Miss Fane's eyes widened as she noticed for the first time the cane that rested by the captain's side and the way he favored his right leg each time the carriage bounced. "I'm sorry," she murmured.

His eyes dancing, Carswell replied, "Why? Because you now cannot bring yourself to abuse me as roundly as before? You need not regard it, you know. Feel free to say whatever you wish, I beg of you."

Miss Fane merely regarded him grimly. Others in the carriage were not so behind, however. "Tell us about your leg, cap'n."

"Aye. 'Ow were you 'urt?"

"Did you know m'boy? Tom Moses? In the Peninsula, 'e was, before the bloody Frenchies killed 'im!"

Carswell answered the last question first. Gravely he replied, "There were a great many of us in the Peninsula, ma'am, and a great many of us killed there. I don't believe I knew your son, but I've no doubt he fought bravely."

The woman thanked him, dabbing at her eyes. Another passenger persisted. "Tell us about it, will you?"

Carswell did, amusing his companions with tales of the resourcefulness of sometimes starving soldiers, misunderstandings caused by poorly spoken Spanish, and a time when he had shared a shelter with three pigs, one goat, and any number of chickens while the rain poured down outside.

Through all of this Miss Fane did not speak. It

was only when they had been set down at Ipswich that she turned to Carswell and asked quietly, "Just how much of that was true, captain?"

A grim look came over his face as he replied curtly, "All of it." He looked at her and his expression softened as he added, "But I did not tell them the rest of it. The mud, the pain, the weariness, the vermin, the fear, the horror of battle, the feelings when one sees that one's now dead enemy was only, after all, still a boy."

Miss Fane found that she wanted to banish the ghosts that seemed to haunt Captain Carswell. Without thinking she put a hand gently on his arm and said, "It is over now."

He looked at her. "For me," he replied grimly. "But not for all the men who have taken my place." Carswell looked away and added roughly, "Oh, to be sure, I haven't any other answers. What can one do when faced with such a man as Napoleon except fight him? But however necessary, nothing can make war anything but horror." He paused at the look on her face and somehow managed a smile. "Never mind. We can talk about that later if you wish. For now we must find the theater in this town and speak to the manager. I do not mean to leave you to face that ordeal alone. Then once we have determined whether or not you have an acting position, we can see to the rest of your needs."

"Plan our campaign, you mean?" Miss Fane rallied him with a smile.

Captain Carswell smiled down at her as well. "Precisely," he said.

With a meekness that surprised herself even more than Captain Carswell, Miss Fane agreed. Anyone who knew her would have been astonished that she made no objection to the high-handed way in which he had taken charge of her immediate future. Which was, Miss Fane grimly told herself later, but one more evidence of the strain on her nerves and also of her extraordinary naiveté!

2

H ENRY Parkins was a man whose habitual expression was one of confidence whatever his inner turmoil. Today's events, however, had managed to penetrate so thoroughly that he now paced the small theater office that was his for as long as the troupe he supervised performed in Ipswich. The cause of his distress was the discovery that the young performer he had most recently acquired for his troupe had not only lied about the death of her guardian but also about her age. And if her guardian made good his threats, Henry Parkins might well find himself facing charges. Only the hope that the genteel family the girl came from would most assuredly wish to avoid scandal kept him from utter despair.

The result of the day's events was such that upon hearing that an applicant had appeared who wished to join the troupe, Henry Parkins was first delighted, then cast into dismay when the young person was ushered into the small office. She looked well enough until she opened her mouth. Then the image created by the shabby clothing she wore gave way to certainty that Miss Fane was a young lady. Whatever the circumstances that had contrived to land her upon his doorstep, Henry Parkins did not want to hear them. After this morning's events, Miss Fane's presence in his acting troupe was a complication Henry Parkins emphatically did not need.

Miss Fane entered the office alone, for Captain Carswell had declined to accompany her further than the stage door. He rather shrewdly guessed that his presence would not aid her chances. And while he thought it unlikely that a career in the theater was in Miss Fane's best interests, he was not such a fool as to believe there might not be worse possibilities should she fail to secure the position. Moreover, he wished to continue in the role of friend to Miss Fane, and should she feel that by his actions he had cost her a job she would be most unlikely to forgive him.

Nevertheless, it was a pity Captain Carswell was unable to be present at the interview for he would have enjoyed it a great deal, as Miss Fane most assuredly did not.

Henry Parkins mopped his brow as he tried to remonstrate with the girl. "I am most sorry, Miss, er, Fane, but I have no positions to offer. None at all. Nor would you be in the least suitible if I did."

"How can you know that?" Miss Fane protested. "You have not even allowed me to read for you. Or sing. Or dance. How can you know what I am or am not capable of? Why won't you give me a chance?"

With the memory of the meeting with his previous ingenue's guardian still so fresh in his mind, Parkins could only continue to remonstrate. "Miss Fane, I am an experienced company manager and I do assure you that when I say you would not suit I know very well what I am talking about."

At last pride reasserted itself and Miss Fane drew herself to her full height, which was just above five feet five, and with flashing gray eyes and a toss of her curling blonde hair she said, "Very well, Mr. Parkins. But when I have become famous upon the London stage I hope you do not regret your impetuous decision this day."

Then, to Mr. Parkins's vast relief she was gone and he sank into the nearest chair, devoutly grateful that his company's tour in Ipswich was almost at an end.

Outside, Captain Carswell came awkwardly to his feet at the sight of Miss Fane's distressed face, for her composure had lasted no farther than the theater door. "You do not have a part in the company," he said, and it was not a question.

Miss Fane looked up at him and suddenly the captain's tall figure with its jet-black hair, wryly smiling face, and sympathetic brown eyes seemed a refuge she dearly needed just now. Propriety kept her from being so indiscreet, however, as to seek comfort against the chest that beckoned so temptingly. Instead, Miss Fane made a great effort to collect herself and said with a watery chuckle, "Oh, I am greatly set down in my conceit. It seems that even without listening to me read or sing or watch me dance the company manager is able to discern that I would be totally unwelcome in his troupe. And here I had thought I need do no more than present myself to be given all the leads, all the choicest parts."

Carswell chuckled in return. "Even if you had been taken on," he said dryly, "I doubt you would have been given the leads. Surely you must know that by tradition they stay with whoever has been performing them. However talented a newcomer might be, there is such a thing as experience to be reckoned with."

Miss Fane shook her head. "I had not known that. It seems there is no end to my naivete," she said with a mock sigh.

Carswell did not miss the lines of distress that marked her face in spite of her attempts at levity. Quietly he said, "I think that you have need of refreshment. Just as I do," he added to forestall her protests. "Perhaps we should return to the inn where we left our baggage and over a meal decide what you are to do next."

"Very well," Miss Fane agreed with unaccustomed meekness.

Carswell did not suggest nor did Miss Fane request a private parlor. They were both content to sit down to a neat luncheon at a table in the common room. When the food had been placed before them Carswell asked casually, "Just how desperate is your situation, Miss Fane?"

She did not at once reply. Instead, she considered the matter carefully. Some months ago she had come to the decision to leave her home. Since then she had saved whatever pin money she could, so that now a respectable sum rested in her reticule. But Miss Fane knew very well it would not last long were she standing the expense of a room at an inn and food. "I must procure a position, but I shall not starve for a while if I do not," Miss Fane said at last.

Carswell nodded approvingly. "Good. Then we may make inquiries to see if there are any families hereabouts who need a girl to work in their household. Unless you would rather return home," he added carelessly.

Grim determination filled Miss Fane, and with a voice that brooked no argument she said, "I am not returning home, Captain Carswell. For reasons that you could not possibly understand, that would be impossible. I must and shall find a position here."

Carswell shrugged and said carelessly. "As you will. It is, after all, of no great moment to me what you do. I simply asked a question."

Anger slowly drained away and at last Miss Fane was able to say, with even a degree of kindness, "Thank you. And I am sorry if I offended you."

"Quite all right," Carswell said amiably. "I've no doubt it is the strain of being on your own, for the first time in your life, with no one to take care of you." She looked at him sharply, but Carswell's expression was all innocence as he went on, "I shudder to think how callow a youth I was when my father first bought my colors, or the amusement I afforded my fellow officers."

"I find that very difficult to imagine," Miss Fane said dryly.

"But it's true," Carswell protested. "They used to say that I was badly in need of a mother hen to watch over me. Perhaps it is that fellow feeling that makes me reluctant to abandon you in your current distress."

"How kind of you," Miss Fane said dryly.

Suspicion was evident in the fine gray eyes the young woman turned on him and Carswell hastened to add, with a sincerity she could not doubt, "I assure you, Miss Fane, I do not mean to take advantage of you. *In any way.* If you wish me to go away, I shall. But I should like to hang about just until I see that you have found a position." He paused, then added gently, "I understand that a

Reverend Watkins means to set up a registry, in London, for female servants. Already he is active in helping them find positions. In his care, or through his agency, at least, you would not need to fear the sorts of abuses that go on elsewhere."

Miss Fane colored. One more evidence, she thought, of her naiveté that she would have assumed all registries honest and secure. Aloud she merely said to him, "You are good to help me without even knowing my story. And without preaching propriety at me."

Carswell regarded her grimly and it was a moment before he replied. "I have seen a great deal," he said at last, "and none of it pretty, in battle. I am not such a fool as to imagine that I can tell you what you must do. As you yourself have pointed out, I cannot know what it is you flee. All I can do is perhaps warn you of some of the dangers you face ahead. And I shall if I can. One of which is being seen too frequently in my company. Therefore, while I shall be about and keeping an eye upon you, I shall not be forever at your side. Good luck and good day, Miss Fane."

And with that, he was gone, leaving Miss Fane to attempt to make sense of what had occurred. In the end she could not, and she settled for arranging for a room for the next several nights and sat down to write letters of inquiry to those houses where the innkeeper assured her the family was in need of a governess. And, true to his word, she did not see Captain Carswell again for the rest of the day. It was foolish, she knew, to depend upon the help of a stranger, but she found herself unaccountably missing Captain Carswell and mourning the loss she would feel when she obtained her position and he moved on.

As for Captain Carswell, he took a short walk through the town, trying to discover just what it was about Miss Fane that made him want to protect her. She was lovely, or rather would have been if she were properly dressed and coiffed, but the captain was accustomed to loveliness. She was young and lonely, but when he had quit the Peninsula, Carswell had promised himself he was done with looking after young and lonely souls, male or female. In the end, however, he knew it didn't matter. What was important was that he had begun to once again care what the days ahead would bring. And to feel curious about another person's troubles.

3

IT was almost a week later that Miss Moira Fane was forced to acknowledge how discouraged she felt. The previous three days of rain had not helped her spirits, but the problem went far beyond that. Of the many letters of inquiry she had sent to prospective employers only one had yielded an interview and that only because Mrs. Matthews was so desperate to find a governess for her seven daughters. Even the dire circumstances that had led her to overlook the irregularity of Miss Fane's application and her lack of references, however, could not win Miss Fane the job once Mrs. Matthews had seen the girl.

"I've two sons and I will *not* expose them to someone as attractive as you are," Mrs. Matthews told Moira bluntly. "Moreover, I do not think you have the stamina to manage seven girls, one of whom is very nearly your own age. I am sorry, but I require a woman not a child. Good day, Miss Fane."

And with that Miss Fane had found herself dismissed and faced with the long walk back into town, since the expenses of maintaining a household with nine children did not allow the Matthewses the luxury of extra carriages or coachmen to ferry servants or potential servants about.

Captain Carswell had told Miss Fane, of course, that she was fortunate not to be hired to work in such an overwhelming household. His vivid description of the horrors Moira would have faced as governess to seven lively girls made her laugh, but in the end even he had not been able to suggest what she was to do instead.

All of this had occurred before the rains began and in the past few days there had not been any jobs or interviews offered at all. Thus, Miss Fane was scarcely in the best of moods as she started on a short walk out toward the countryside and away from the busy streets of Ipswich. It was the first clear day that had dawned and Miss Fane meant to make the most of it. Captain Carswell was nowhere to be seen, but Moira had by now become accustomed to his absences. Besides, she was grimly determined not to become dependent upon his kindness, or his steadfastness, or his advice. She must learn to make her way alone. It occurred to Miss Fane, not for the first time, that perhaps she should go to London and try the agency Captain Carswell had recommended there.

Because Miss Fane was so deep in thought, she did not notice the curricle that drew up along side her until it halted and the gentleman driving tossed the reins to his groom and jumped down from it. "Hallo!" he said in an admiring tone of voice. "May I know your name?"

"I beg your pardon," Miss Fane said blankly. "Are you speaking to me?"

"I most certainly am," the fellow retorted with

something akin to a leer. "I've always rather fancied provincial roses. Come, tell me your name."

Miss Fane might have been naive but she was scarcely an utter fool. Hastily she looked about. The road was not entirely deserted, but no one was yet paying any attention to herself or the gentleman. As for him, he looked to be a man without any scruples. Certainly the lines of dissipation about his face argued that he had lived a decadent life thus far. Nevertheless, Moira managed to say coolly, "If you don't leave me alone, sir, I shall scream."

A hard look replaced the leer on the gentleman's face and he straightened. "Shall you indeed?" he asked just as coolly. "How interesting. And if I simply cover your mouth and abduct you? Will your outraged family come running? I assure you, I've the money to buy them off."

"I doubt it," Miss Fane retorted bravely.

"Shall we try and see?" the gentleman suggested lazily.

There was nothing lazy, however, in the way he reached for her or the strength of the arms that held her and pulled her toward the curricle. Miss Fane scarcely had time to think. She bit the hand clamped over her mouth and brought her heel down as hard as she could upon his foot, but it was not sufficient to make him release her.

Then, suddenly, she was free and the gentleman lay on the ground with Carswell standing over him, cane in hand. In a bored tone of voice Carswell addressed the fellow on the ground and said, "You will do best to leave this woman alone."

"As you have not?" the gentleman asked with a sneer as he rose and brushed himself off. To his disappointment, Carswell refused to be baited but merely stood there. The gentleman climbed into his curricle, took the reins from his groom, and added in a silkily dangerous voice, "This is no woman, however, but a young lady. In that I cannot be mistaken. Her appearance argues much irregularity in her behavior and I mean to discover who she is. When I do, my dear," he said directly to Miss Fane, "I venture to predict you will greatly regret it. Good day to both of you."

Only when he was far down the road did Miss Fane let out her breath in a deep sigh. "Precisely," Captain Carswell agreed grimly. "Let us hope he is not planning an extended stay in Ipswich."

Miss Fane fervently agreed. They started back toward the inn, Captain Carswell leaning heavily on his cane. When they got there, they found the Vicar of Ipswich waiting for them. "I've just had a visit from the Marquess of Alnwick and he informed me of matters I can no longer ignore," the vicar told the pair. "I am here to tell you that I hope you are prepared either to be married or to be out of town within the next few hours," he said in an implacable voice.

Miss Fane and Captain Carswell looked at one another blankly, then at the vicar. He regarded them with a grimness that was untouched by the least trace of compassion. Inexorably he went on, "I have watched the pair of you for the past week trying to make up my mind. You have been discreet, I will grant you that, and so far as I can discover, you, Miss Fane, have made an attempt to obtain legitimate employ. But I can stand aside no longer. The gentleman who came to see me was quite correct in saying that something quite irregular is going on here, and I will not allow it. If you are not prepared to be married, then I wish both of you to leave Ipswich at once. Mrs. Matthews has already spoken to me of the danger you represent to the young men of this town, Miss Fane."

"Don't you even wish to hear Miss Fane's story," Captain Carswell asked mildly.

"No," the vicar said, shaking his head. "Whatever it is, I don't want to hear it, I simply want both of you married or both of you gone before you corrupt any of my flock."

And with that the small vicar turned on his heel and strode away in the direction of his church. "Well," Captain Carswell said with a sigh, "I think we had best go and see when the next mail coach comes through town."

"He can't make us go, surely," Miss Fane protested angrily, and began to pace about the common room. "Or get married, can he?"

Another sigh, this time of exasperation, escaped the captain. "No, he can't make us go," Carswell agreed, "but he can make things damned unpleasant for us while we stay, and he can guarantee you won't find a position here. What respectable family do you think is going to hire you if the vicar says they are not to? Or are you so foolhardy as to be prepared to work for a family that is not respectable?"

Reluctantly, Miss Fane nodded. When he was satisfied that she had indeed subdued her temper he asked coolly, "Well, where do you go next, Miss Fane? For which mail coach am I to be inquiring?"

Her voice faltered but she met his eyes squarely as she said, "I don't know."

Again Carswell waited before he spoke. "That fellow who approached you was the Marquess of

Alnwick. The same fellow who spoke to the vicar. And he meant what he said, you know. That he was going to find out who you are and that he was going to cause you trouble. He has a reputation for such things. Don't you think I ought to know who you are first?"

In a burst of anger Miss Fane said, "The Marquess of Alnwick also told me he would abduct me and buy off my family if they didn't like it."

"And what did you reply?" Carswell asked mildly.

"I told me he couldn't do it," Miss Fane said with some satisfaction.

"No, they wouldn't be bought off, would they?" Carswell said thoughtfully. "Not if they are like any other family I've ever met. They would be far more likely to insist that you marry him to salvage your reputation, wouldn't they? And he is unmarried, you know."

Miss Fane met his eyes in dismay. "You're right, they would!" she gasped.

"Which is one reason why I think you should tell me who you are so that I can know how best to help you. And don't—" he held up a hand in warning— "tell me any more Banbury tales about being someone named Miss Moira Fane."

"How do I know I can trust you any more than I could trust him?" Miss Fane asked accusingly.

"You don't," Captain Carswell replied coolly. "Of course, the fact that I have not tried to ravish you this past week might be something in my favor, but on the other hand it might simply mean I play a more subtle game. Assure me that you are going to return to your family and I shall happily let you go without knowing a thing more about you," he said, lying without the least compunction.

"I can't go home," she said resolutely.

"To relatives, then?" he suggested. She hesitated and he pressed the point. "Even relatives you don't know well. If you are in trouble, surely they would be honor-bound to help you."

"I don't know," she said slowly.

Captain Carswell swung Miss Fane around to face him. Still holding her arms he said, all trace of mockery gone now, "Then tell me. Tell me what you've run from and who you might run to, and between us perhaps we may come to a solution. You're right when you say that you've no reason to trust me, and God knows I should be glad you've finally the sense to be suspicious of everyone, including me. But in spite of that, I swear to you I would never hurt you."

For several moments Miss Fane did not answer. Then, at last, she said quietly, "My name is Mary Farnham. I've run away from home because my father died when I was ten and my mother soon remarried, and for many reasons I could not get along with my stepfather or he with me. Nor his children from his first wife. And so, in the end, I determined to run away."

"Because you disliked your stepfamily?" Carswell asked incredulously.

Mary Farnham shook her head and swallowed before she answered. In a small voice he could scarcely hear she told him, "No, it is far more than that, but I beg of you not to press me to tell you the rest."

"Very well," Carswell replied grimly.

"Oh, thank you," she said, relief evident in her eyes.

Sternly he added, "At any rate, I shan't press you now. But we have to find an answer as to where you are to go. What about relatives?"

Miss Farnham shook her head. "I've not seen any of them since my father died. Mother didn't get along with them, hers or his, and my stepfather even less so." She paused, then added, "I have an Aunt Gwendolyn and Uncle Hubert who came to visit once and I liked them very much. I even wanted to grow up to be just like her. But that was ten years ago and I'm not sure they remember me anymore."

"Where do they live?" Carswell asked gently.

"Brighton," Miss Farnham replied. "At least during the summer."

"Then I suggest we go to Brighton," Carswell said curtly. At her start of surprise he added, "Why not? We've got to go somewhere, and we've nothing to lose. If your aunt and uncle turn their backs on you, then we simply go somewhere else."

"But your own travels," Miss Farnham protested. "Surely you've wasted enough time on mine?"

Once more, grimness touched Carswell's face as he replied, "I assure you, Miss Farnham, it is no hardship to me. I've no set course, no fixed destination. Like you, I don't wish to be at home."

"And where is home?" Miss Farnham asked quietly.

But Carswell did not answer. He simply limped away.

CAPTAIN Carswell assisted Miss Farnham down from the mail coach and looked about him. The busy courtyard of the inn bustled with activity and any number of young urchins wishing to make a few pence carrying baggage. Captain Carswell spoke to a group of sturdy-looking fellows, gave the name they sought, and said, "Do any of you know the family? Or where they live?"

"I do, sir," one lad replied quickly. "You'll be wanting a cab, I expect," he added, looking at the captain's cane.

Carswell nodded but stopped the boy as he started to pick up the baggage. "Wait a moment. Can you recommend a good inn? Not too expensive, but quiet and clean?"

"Right, I can, sir. The Horn and Hare caters to Quality, it does, but don't cost a fortune like some I could name."

"Good lad!" Carswell said approvingly. "You can take my bags there and tell them to expect me in a little while. After I have escorted this lady to her aunt and uncle."

As these instructions were accompanied by a

half crown and the promise of another when
Carswell returned to the inn, the boy acted with
immediate goodwill to do so. When Miss Farnham
suggested, in the cab, that the captain might be
fortunate were his bags not to disappear, Carswell
laughed. "No fear of that," he said. "The boy will
want the other half crown. But more than that,
when one has traveled, as I have, in the harum-
scarum of war, one learns how to read faces and
discover who may be trusted and who will run off
with one's things."

"I hope you may be right," Miss Farnham said
gravely, which only caused the captain to laugh
again.

Not ten minutes later they were climbing the
steps to the Brighton household belonging to
Hubert Foster and his wife Gwendolyn. The
footman who opened the door could not entirely
suppress his surprise at sight of the baggage set
down by the coachman at Miss Farnham's feet. "I
shall fetch Mrs. Foster immediately," he
stammered upon hearing Mary's name, and then
rudely left them standing in the hall.

"Perhaps we ought to simply sneak back out the
door," Miss Farnham suggested apprehensively.

"Nonsense!" Carswell retorted. "Never retreat
unless absolutely necessary. Why, we have not
even determined yet if your aunt is friend or foe."

Grimly, Carswell promised himself that if the
aunt should prove foe he would favor her with a
number of pungent, well chosen words before he
took Miss Farnham away. The first sight of Mrs.
Foster reassured him, however. She came toward
them without the least trace of dismay upon her
face. Indeed, she smiled at the pair and said easily,
"Mary, my dear, how are you! How was your

journey? You must forgive me, for you know how
wretched my memory is and I completely forgot to
tell the servants to prepare your room! Even
worse, I have forgotten the name of this gentleman
whom your mother said was going to bring you."

Rising admirably to the occasion Miss Farnham
replied coolly, "This is Captain Carswell, of
course, Aunt Gwendolyn. Captain Carswell, my
aunt, Mrs. Foster."

"How do you do?' he said, executing a neat bow
in spite of his injured leg.

Mrs. Foster smiled and inclined her head. "Shall
we go upstairs to my sitting room? I have guests in
the drawing room and I know you must be too
tired after your journey to wish to be civil to
strangers." To the footman she added, "James,
please have my niece's bags taken up to the pink
bedroom and tell Mrs. Williams she is here."

"Yes, ma'am."

Mrs. Foster led the way and none of the three
spoke until they were safely ensconced behind a
closed door. Then she turned and faced them,
indicated that she expected them to sit down, and
finally said grimly, "That ought to scotch the
worst of the gossip, but I want to know what is
going on and I want to know right now! Who are
you, Captain Carswell, and what are you doing
with my niece?"

"Merely escorting her into your care, ma'am,"
he replied meekly.

"That doesn't tell me who you are," Mrs. Foster
reminded him.

Captain Carswell looked up at the woman facing
him. She was still relatively young, he judged, not
above five and thirty. She was taller than Miss
Farnham but with the same clear gray eyes staring

out at him from below a head of hair only slightly darker than her niece's. There was intelligence in those eyes and even a hint of amusement. Perhaps that was what decided him to tell her the truth. "My name is Randall Carswell," he said quietly, "and I am the younger son of Lord Atley, and I have just a few months past sold out my commission in the Hussars due to injuries."

Mrs. Foster's eyes lingered a moment on his cane, then she acknowledged his answer with a nod of her head and turned to Miss Farnham. "Well, Mary?" she asked.

The girl met her aunt's eyes squarely. "You know Mama. And her husband. I couldn't stay there any longer."

"So you came straight here. Without writing first? And somehow acquired Captain Carswell on the way?" Mrs. Foster asked coolly.

"No. I ran away and tried to join a traveling theater troupe in Ipswich, but they wouldn't have me," Mary replied frankly. "I encountered Captain Carswell on the mail coach and he has been kind enough to look after me, even rescuing me from an importunate gentleman."

"The Marquess of Alnwick," Carswell added helpfully. Mrs. Foster once more turned her piercing gaze on the captain and he said innocently, "Our behavior was beyond reproach, I assure you. But I simply could not leave the child to make her way on her own; she is far too naive. And I had nothing better to do, at the time."

Mrs. Foster's lips twitched but she remained silent and Mary hastened to say, "It's true, Aunt Gwendolyn. Indeed, he is the one who insisted I must stop trying to get a position as a governess or something and come to see you instead. You won't try to send me home, will you?"

"To that household? I should think not!" Mrs. Foster replied in withering accents. "Very well, I shall take it as given, then, Mary, that you have done nothing to ruin yourself. The story shall be that Captain Carswell is an acquaintance of the family and was kind enough to escort you here at your mother's request. I shall write and inform her of that at once. She is not such a nodcock as to refuse to go along with the story. After all, she cannot wish to have people asking why you were so unhappy as to run away. And as for why you have come to visit me, no one will find it in the least strange that you grew tired of the country-side and wished to finally have a taste of society."

"Yes, Aunt Gwendolyn," Mary said meekly.

Mrs. Foster was not deceived. "Excellent. You must cultivate precisely that manner," she said dryly to her niece, "and then we shall have no trouble finding you a husband."

"To aid which event you no doubt wish I will disappear," Captain Carswell suggested innocently.

Shrewd gray eyes studied him a moment before Mrs. Foster said thoughtfully, "Not at once, I should hope. That would cause talk. Far better if you would be kind enough to stay in Brighton a few days so that nothing looks havey-cavey. Come to call, perhaps go to dinner with my husband Hubert, that sort of thing. Play the part of an old family friend."

It was Carswell's turn to study the ladies. After a moment he shrugged lazily and said, "As you wish."

"Good," Mrs. Foster said decisively. "And now I

must go back down to my other guests before they wonder what I am about. Mary, I should like you to follow me as soon as you have changed your traveling dress and washed up a bit. That will give me time to prepare them. Captain Carswell, I regret that I must ask you to leave. However kind you have been in looking after my niece, she is now in my care and I must have a regard for her reputation. You may come to call tomorrow morning. Indeed, we shall quite expect you. Good day."

Captain Carswell did not take offense. Quite the contrary. He rose and bowed amiably to both ladies, agreed to call the next day, then said to Miss Farnham, "I see why you told me you once wanted to grow up to be like your aunt. And I see where you have your talent for acting from. She is delightful."

Mrs. Foster snorted. "Brassy. Managing. Far too independent-minded, these I might allow, Captain Carswell. But *delightful*? Surely that is doing it much too brown."

"Not in the least!" was the captain's outrageous reply.

Mrs. Foster went on as though she had not heard him. "As for my acting, well, I do not like to lie. But we live in a society that worships propriety, or rather the appearance of propriety, over common sense. I am not about to sacrifice my niece to that."

"As I said before, you are delightful," Carswell repeated, and then he exited the room, managing to do so gracefully in spite of his limp.

Once more Mrs. Foster laughed. She turned to her niece and said shrewdly, "Now that is a man worth knowing, my dear. I applaud your taste, if not your discretion. But," she added severely, "now we had both best exercise a bit of the latter if we are to carry off your presence here. Go and change and meet me downstairs as soon as you may. There should be a maidservant waiting in your room to help you. She can show you the way to the drawing room."

"Yes, Aunt Gwendolyn," Mary said meekly.

She followed her aunt out the door and to her own room, grateful that her arrival had come off so smoothly. Perhaps everything would work out after all. Meanwhile, if she remembered correctly, there was a pretty sprigged muslin dress somewhere in her trunk.

Half an hour later she stood in the doorway of her aunt's drawing room dressed in the sprigged muslin with her hair coiled charmingly atop her head, ringlets escaping artfully to frame her face. Looking up, Gwendolyn Foster could not help but approve the modest way Mary waited for her to speak. "Ah, Lady Crane, here is my niece now. Mary, come in, girl, and make your curtsy." To her friend she added, "You must know that my sister-in-law has been so busy with her small ones that she has been unable to bring Mary out, and so I have begged the favor of doing so. First here in Brighton so that she may acquire a bit of polish, and then next spring in London. Mary is a good girl, attractive as you can see, and something of an heiress, so I am hopeful she will not find herself entirely a wallflower."

Lady Crane pronounced herself charmed, promised to bring her own daughter round to meet Mary, and asked all manner of kind questions about her journey. Gwendolyn was pleased to note that without actually lying Mary

managed to answer and not betray that anything
irregular had occurred.

At that point Hubert Foster appeared in the
doorway of the drawing room. Gwendolyn cast
her husband an anxious look, but she need not
have worried. He came forward and engulfed his
niece in a warm hug of welcome before he stepped
back and said, "Well, well, so you've arrived at
last, my dear. I am delighted to see you. I trust
your journey was a pleasant one? Good, good. We
shall talk about it later, I am just come in from my
club and have some papers to attend to.
Gwendolyn, m'love, I came to tell you that I shall
be dining at home tonight, after all."

Gwendolyn acknowledged this information with
a nod of her head and an affectionate smile,
heedless of the disapproving look of her friend
Lady Crane. There were those who might call her
brassy and shockingly independent, but Hubert
had never been one of them. His intelligence easily
matched her own and just as he was not a man to
be controlled by any woman, neither did he try to
dictate to Gwendolyn. What had begun as a match
between two reckless, infatuated children, had
grown over the years into a deep, abiding
closeness between two friends as well as lovers.
That this fact was a cause of gossip and surprise
among the *ton* said more about the marriages of
others than about their own.

Perhaps their only regret over the years was
that they seemed unable to have children. Now
Gwendolyn was at last breeding and she had her
niece to look after as well! Which was very nice,
only what was she to do once she started showing?
It would not be *comme-il-faut* for her to chaperone
the girl about then. But as it was not a part of

Gwendolyn's nature to fret over what she could not change, she turned her attention back to Lady Crane and left such worries to the future.

5

CAPTAIN Carswell did call as requested the next morning. He stayed the correct half hour, was polite to Mrs. Foster's other guests, then left without saying when he would next visit. Indeed, his manner toward Miss Farnham was noted to be almost avuncular and he appeared to be paying a duty call rather than one of pleasure.

Two mornings later, however, when Captain Carswell called, there was nothing apathetic about his manner. He presented himself at the Foster household and asked impatiently to speak with Mrs. Foster alone. Much to his relief, she did not keep him waiting long but soon arrived in the bookroom where Captain Carswell had asked the footman to place him. Mrs. Foster took one searching look at his face, then closed the door of the bookroom behind her and came forward. "Please sit down, captain," she said kindly. "I collect you have something important to say to me, but we may as well be comfortable. Now how may I help you?"

Carswell started to protest but changed his mind and meekly took the seat indicated. "I've come to say good-bye, Mrs. Foster. Later, in a day or two, will you tell Miss Farnham I have gone?"

Mrs. Foster leaned back in her chair and regarded her guest with shrewd eyes. "A problem has come up at home, perhaps?" she suggested mildly. "Or perhaps you mean to tell me you are required on urgent business in London?"

"No, no, none of that," Carswell retorted irritably. "I simply have decided to leave Brighton."

"Without saying good-bye to my niece," Mrs. Foster said kindly. "Come, will you tell me what the difficulty is?"

"Surely that is evident to you?" Carswell said in exasperation. "My presence in Brighton, hanging about your niece, will do her no good. She ought to be looking about her for a husband. And now that Miss Farnham is in safe hands, she has no need of me."

"Yet you were quite ready to stay, two days ago," Mrs. Foster pointed out gently.

Carswell rose stiffly to his feet and began to pace the small room, leaning on his cane as he did so. "That was before I discovered that Miss Farnham is an heiress!" he said, bitterness tinging the words. "Neither you nor she saw fit to mention that to me."

"Does it matter?" Mrs. Foster asked mildly.

Carswell paused and looked at her, absently running a hand through his dark curly locks as he did so. "I have no wish to be taken for a fortune hunter," he said with great precision. "And we both know I can be no acceptable suitor for your niece, not under the circumstances."

"How—how odd," a voice came from behind them, "I had not thought you a man overly given to caring what society said. Or that anyone considered you a suitor for my hand."

"Mary!"

"Miss Farnham!"

The voices spoke in unison and apparently Miss Farnham felt constrained to answer, for she shut the door behind her and came forward. Facing Carswell she said forthrightly, "James said you were here and I naturally assumed it was to see both my aunt and myself. It seems I was mistaken. Forgive me. But I will say, before I go, that what I overheard seems arrant nonsense to me. There is no question of anyone calling you a fortune hunter, because there is no danger of anyone thinking your behavior in the least to mean you were dangling after me. It is the . . . the most absurd notion in the world. It must be evident to anyone who sees us together that you consider me little more than a nuisance, so I cannot see what it is that you fear."

Carswell's face had changed color nearly as often as Miss Farnham's during this little speech and did so again as he asked quietly, "Why did you not tell me you were an heiress? You know very well I thought you an impoverished vicar's daughter, or some such thing."

Mary brushed past him and stood by the window. It was several moments before she answered with a shrug, "Why, how should I have thought you would care? If you were, as you seemed, simply a disinterested, kindly protector, what should it matter? And if you were a scoundrel, why then it might simply have given you reason to try to abduct me. Perhaps I did not care to put you to the test."

Mrs. Foster, who had been watching both of

them with great interest, now spoke. "Or perhaps my niece correctly judged that you would be put off by the news," she said to Carswell. "But in any event, Mary is quite right. You are sufficiently older than my niece for the idea that you were pursuing her to seem absurd. I am certain you need not fear that anyone in the *ton* will think so."

Mrs. Foster noted with satisfaction that her words had once more caused the captain to change color. She went on with deceptive meekness, "We have no right to ask you to alter your plans for our convenience, of course, but I did hope you would stay in Brighton just a trifle longer. My niece, you see, has spoken of trying to join an acting troupe here and somehow I had thought you might have more success in dissuading her from going upon the stage than I have."

"What the devil?" Captain Carswell exploded in rage. Just whom he was most angry at was not entirely clear even in his own mind. "You are roasting me, of course, madam. Now that Miss Farnham is in your care, I find it very difficult to believe she would continue to envision such nonsense as trying to go upon the stage," he said, looking from one to the other.

"Nonsense!" Mary confronted him, her eyes flashing in anger and disbelief. "Why should it be nonsense? Do you consider the alternative any better? That I should be dependent upon my aunt and uncle for all my needs? For how long? Certainly my own mother and stepfather are not about to set me up in my own household, and I do not inherit until I am twenty-five this fortune everyone is so afraid of."

"I am not afraid of it," Gwendolyn Foster

pointed out meekly, but no one paid attention to her.

"You should get married," Carswell thundered at Mary.

"Oh, really," she replied sweetly, "why? So that I may become a possession of my husband? Or so that I may have children? I have not observed that they gave my mother any happiness. Or perhaps you think I cannot take care of myself. But that is only true if I give a fig for my reputation. Life becomes very simple if I cast propriety to the winds, as I am strongly tempted to do."

"You little fool!" Carswell told her bluntly. "There are far worse things to be afraid of than simply the loss of your reputation. As you will soon find out if you are so foolish as to pursue this notion of going upon the stage!"

Gwendolyn Foster glanced from one to the other and smiled. Smoothly, she rose to her feet and said, "If you will excuse me, there are some matters I must attend to. I shall be back shortly."

Almost absent-mindedly, they watched her go, neither Mary nor Carswell thinking of how unconventional Mrs. Foster's behavior must be.

Instead, they continued to glare at one another. At last Mary said, a trifle petulantly, "It is none of your affair, after all, what I do."

Captain Carswell leaned against one of the bookcases that lined the walls of the room and set the cane against it as well. "Very true," he said coolly. "The matter is not, however, one of indifference to your aunt. She has, I collect, been quite kind in taking you in and it would scarcely serve her a good turn if you were to launch yourself upon the stage straight from her household. You may not care a fig for your reputation, but

I've yet to see that she is similarly careless of her own.''

Miss Farnham paled, swallowed, then said quietly, ''That is the one reason I have not yet gone to the theater to arrange an audition. Somehow, I must disguise who I am. Aunt Gwendolyn can simply say I've gone back home again.''

''Unless, of course, you and I both disappear from Brighton at the same time. *Then* your Aunt Gwendolyn would have some difficulty preventing the conjecture that we both left together,'' Carswell observed mildly. ''But as you are not going upon the stage, the problem does not after all exist,'' he added, his eyes fixed upon Mary's face.

''You cannot stop me,'' she taunted him.

With an oath Carswell took a stride forward, forgetting his leg, and placed strong hands upon Mary Farnham's shoulders. ''No?'' he demanded, shaking her. ''If I find you have been so abominable as to do so, I shall come straight back to Brighton, put you across my knees, and give you the thrashing you so richly deserve. And let me tell you, my dear, that I am astonished that no one has done so before!''

''How dare you?'' Mary hissed at him. ''You did not think my plans so absurd in Ipswich.''

Carswell let go of her shoulders. ''In Ipswich,'' he said, ''I did not know what you were running from or that you had anywhere to run to. I thought your plans absurd but could well believe that the alternatives open to you were worse. Now, however, I find that you have a loving aunt to take care of you, a fortune to inherit in what, six years? And you still mean to ruin yourself. Well, my girl, I will not stand by and let you take risks you cannot possibly understand when there is not the slightest need."

"Ooooh, I wish I were a man!" Mary flung at him.

Carswell deliberately let his eyes wander up and down Miss Farnham's slender figure. His gaze seemed to pierce the thin fabric of her pink cambric gown. More, he lightly fingered a lock of her fair hair, causing her to shiver with anticipation before he said dryly, "Now that would be a pity, bewcause you make such a beautiful young woman."

Then, in spite of all he knew about propriety, in spite of all his best resolutions, in spite of every ounce of common sense he possessed, Captain Carswell reached forward and drew Miss Farnham to him and began to kiss her gently on the lips.

A loud cough behind the pair startled them into jumping apart. A grim look upon her face, Gwendolyn Foster came forward. "Well, Captain Carswell? Do you mean to remain in Brighton a little longer? Without, I hope, a repetition of what has just occurred?"

He colored, then bowed to Mrs. Foster, groped for his cane, and said curtly, "You win. I shall stay in Brighton a little longer. Without a repetition of such behavior, I assure you. Don't imagine, however, that I will enjoy doing so. As for you, Miss Farnham, I meant what I said. If you dare to try anything so outrageous as to go upon the stage, you shall have to answer to me. And now, ladies, good day."

In long, limping strides Carswell reached the door of the bookroom and opened it. As soon as he was gone Miss Farnham sank into the nearest chair and promptly burst into tears. Far from being shocked or distressed, however, it is to be noted that a small smile played about the corner of Mrs. Foster's mouth and her eyes danced a trifle as she watched her niece, waiting patiently for the tears to subside. When she finally spoke, it was to note, mildly, "Captain Carswell appears to have taken your welfare to heart, my dear."

"To heart?" Mary fairly spat out the words in disbelief. "He thinks me the greatest nuisance in the world and while he has somehow managed to convince himself that my welfare is his responsibility, I have no doubt he would be quite happy were he never to set eyes on me again!"

"I see," Mrs. Foster said gravely. "That, of course, is why he so far forgot himself as to kiss you. And do you, er, mean to disobey him in the matter of the theater troupe?"

Miss Farnham started to answer but then shivered and said wryly, "I don't know. He has no right to forbid me, of course, but somehow I am not eager to arouse his anger like that again." She paused and turned troubled eyes upon her aunt. "Nor do I want to cause you any distress, Aunt Gwendolyn. You have been so kind to me."

Mrs. Foster waved a hand carelessly. "That is the least of your worries, my dear. If you were happy, I wouldn't give a fig for the question of reputation—yours or mine. But Captain Carswell was right in saying there were other dangers attached to joining the theater. It is not fair or right, but it is so that gentlemen and men who are not gentlemen are inclined to consider any female on the stage as fair game for whatever they wish to do with her, regardless of how she feels in the matter. Even the captain seemed to believe he had a right to kiss you."

Mary looked away, conscious of an obstruction in her throat as she tried to reply. "He didn't mean anything by it," she said a trifle bitterly. "He merely meant to teach me a lesson, you see."

Gwendolyn Foster thought that she saw very well what had gone on, but she did not dispute the matter with her niece. Instead, she went on talking about the theater. "Being an actress is not as easy a life as it might seem, my dear. Nor is it one that generally pays well. You would, I fear, find it quite insufficient for your needs unless you were both the star and fortunate enough to have a manager who actually paid you your wages."

"Paid me my wages?" Mary asked in confusion, "But wouldn't he have to?"

"It is common knowledge that even the great Mrs. Siddons, for years, was not paid by Mr. Sheridan. And Drury Lane was not precisely an impoverished provincial theater."

Perhaps more than any other argument yet advanced, this news gave pause to Mary Farnham's plans. Mrs. Foster did not press the point but merely allowed her niece time to think it over. After several moments she rose and said briskly, "It is as I said before, my dear, the choice must be yours, however strongly I may feel in the matter. But now we've an appointment with the dressmaker and had best hurry. Do go and fetch your bonnet, I pray you, my dear."

In something of a daze, Mary did as she was bid. By the time she returned downstairs, however, she had shaken off her malaise. Any twinges of guilt she felt over her aunt's spending so much money on her were soon brushed away by that kind lady's genuine protestations that she enjoyed doing so. And even Mary was not proof against the temptations of, for once in her life, having new dresses and shoes and furbelows without having to hear that they were wasted on so ungrateful a child as herself!

6

CAPTAIN Carswell was still in something of a temper when he reached the Horn and Hare. There he encountered an old friend, however, who hailed him. "Carswell! It is you, isn't it? So this is where you've gone to ground. We did wonder, you know. Once you sold out, no one quite knew where you were, except that it was not London."

Very deliberately Carswell turned and frostily eyed the person who had spoken, but it was no use. One look at the twinkling eyes and gangling figure that confronted him and Carswell's own mouth turned itself up into a grin. "Langley, what the devil are you doing here?" he demanded.

"Where else should I be?" the fellow retorted holding his arms out wide. "London is deserted, you know I haven't the taste for Bath, and at least there is some hope of entertainment here in Brighton. Have you been to the theater yet? There is one actress there who is extraordinary. She has the most delightful legs you have ever seen!"

This reminder, coming so soon upon the heels of Miss Farnham's shocking notion, returned the grim look to Carswell's face. "I am afraid," he said curtly, "that I have lost my taste for the theater, of late."

Langley raised his quizzing glass and looked at his friend through it for a long moment before he said, blinking, "Turned to stone, have you? Or lost your heart to a Puritan, perhaps? Maybe we were wrong in thinking the worst damage was to your leg, perhaps your wits were addled instead."

In spite of himself Carswell laughed and clapped his friend on the shoulder with his free hand. "No, just a fit of the megrims, I'm afraid. But come, I tell you what, I'll let you drag me off to the theater this very afternoon, and who knows? Perhaps I'll recover the instant I see those marvelous legs."

"Good fellow!" Langley retorted. "And we'll have to round up Jack and Freddy, too."

"What? Are they in Brighton as well?" Carswell demanded incredulously. "Have you all sold out?"

Langley looked about him quickly to be sure the street was deserted before he replied, "Not precisely. That is, Freddy sold out because his father died and he was the heir. Jack and I, however, are merely here on leave."

"Leave?" Carswell asked doubtfully.

"Well, cooling our heels, at any rate," Langley said ruefully, "and *apparently* on leave. I can't tell you any more than that, but you know Wellington enough to guess the rest."

Carswell nodded curtly. "I should like to say that you might call upon me for any help you need, but I am afraid I could not be of the slightest use to you, these days."

This latter was said with the merest gesture toward his leg. Langley snorted in disgust. "Come now, Carswell, you're not the man to dwell in self-pity. Wasn't it you who gave that young boy in the Peninsula a tongue lashing for grumbling that he had lost an arm? Wasn't it you who told him to be grateful that he was not going home blind or legless or shocked into being little more than a vegetable?"

"Yes, but I find that I am far better at giving advice than at taking it," Carswell said wryly. "Perhaps I am more in need of a visit to that theater than I thought."

"Good," Langley said with a grin. "And while we're on our way, there is something I want to talk to you about."

It was not, as Langley confided loudly to a mutual friend later that evening in one of Brighton's better taverns, that Randall Carswell was unable to handle adversity. Six years of fighting Napoleon had proven he could. No, the problem went far deeper and touched not a little upon the matter of a father and brother who considered him a useless scapegrace despite all of the evidence to the contrary.

"What I don't understand," Jack said with a frown, "is why Headquarters didn't find some use for him. They must know damned well he's a capable man, bad leg or not!"

Langley ordered both of them another drink, then he replied, "Perhaps they did know it and offered Randall a post. You know as well as I do how stiff-necked he is. If he thought there was any hint of pity in the offer, he'd have turned it down in a flash."

"That's true," Jack agreed quietly. "But I still think it a shocking waste. Fact is, he could be doing our job a damned sight better than we are, right now. What say we recruit him to help?"

Langley shook his head. "I tried. You saw how it was, Jack. Randall had as good a time as any of us at the theater matinee. Ogled the girls just as much. But there was a distance there, a reserve I've never seen before. And when I tried to sound him out in the matter of helping us he cut me short, told me he knew well enough what I was hinting at, and to stop being such a gudgeon. As much as told me that he'd had enough of war and thinking about war and would be much obliged if I would just shut up."

"That doesn't sound like Randall," Jack said with another frown.

"I agree, unless he is playing his own game, however unlikely that seems," Langley said. "But then, who knows what we would sound like if we were invalided out."

"True enough," Jack conceded, and they silently drank a toast to Carswell.

Langley had had enough of pessimism, however. Gradually a twinkle came to his eyes and he said thoughtfully, "Of course, the other possibility is that our friend has fallen in love."

"Randall?" Jack snorted in disbelief. "That's even more unlikely. Cuts a fine figure with the ladies, when he chooses, but I've never known him to give more than a passing thought to any one of them."

"Well, if the latest gossip is to be believed, he's given more than that to a Miss Farnham," Langley pointed out.

"To be sure. He escorted an old family friend to Brighton and you've got him half wed already," Jack retorted in withering tones.

Langley gazed at the fire speculatively. "I know, I know," he conceded, "it does seem damned unlikely."

"Particularly when you think how he all but bit off your head for mentioning her name," Jack pointed out.

"At, but that's precisely it," Langley replied, his dancing eyes coming to rest on his friend. "Have you ever known Randall to get that angry over a lady before? Or care whether his name was linked with hers or not?"

That silenced Jack. Almost: All he said was, "If Randall is taken with the girl, I'm devilish glad we've a front-row seat to watch the fun!"

Meanwhile, Carswell was proceeding to get as drunk as it was possible for him to get in one of the less reputable inns in Brighton. Had any of his friends asked him why that inn, he would have replied that while he needed to become castaway, he had no desire to make a fool of himself in front of people who were likely to see him again. Or, he might have added silently, where word might somehow get back to Miss Farnham or the Fosters. The thought of her delightful, angry face was the one thing capable of bringing a smile to his at this moment. Which was, perhaps, just as well considering the touchy nature of the crowd about him now.

Unfortunately for Carswell's wish to go unnoticed, he had the great misfortune to encounter Mr. Foster, some hours later, as he was reeling toward his hotel in the company of two new-found friends. Though they had not yet been formally introduced, Mr. Foster had made it his business to discover just what his niece's erstwhile rescuer looked like and even in the early hours of the morning he knew he was not mistaken in recognizing the fellow. "Good God, is that you, Carswell?" he demanded in astonishment.

With great effort Carswell forced himself upright and blinked, trying to focus his eyes upon the person who had spoken. After a moment he shrugged and said, "Deepest apologies, and all that, but it appears I've forgotten your name."

"Mr. Foster," that gentleman snapped in return, "Mr. Hubert Foster."

"Oh, Lord!" Carswell groaned. "Now I've dished myself, haven't I?" To his companions he said, in his slurred, drunken speech, "Want you to meet a capital fellow. Mr. Hebert Fuster. No, no, that's not right. Mr. Hubert Foster."

The two men, almost as drunk as Carswell, managed clumsy bows without relinquishing their supportive hold on Carswell. "Delighted," they said, or something of the sort.

"I'd introduce you," Carswell persisted, "but I've forgotten my friends' names."

"Names are not important," one of the fellows said hastily.

"What is a name among friends?" the other agreed amiably.

Foster, who was no fool, disliked the looks of Carswell's companions and his profound desire was to turn his back on all three of them. But he was an honorable man and if Mary was to be believed, they owed a debt of gratitude to the fellow, something Foster found very difficult to credit at that moment. Nevertheless, he said, a hint of steel to his voice, "I fear you have forgotten, Carswell, that you were pledged to spend a part of the evening with me. Come. I shall escort you back to your hotel. Now. The two of us alone. I've some business I wish to discuss with you, however ill prepared you are to respond in your present condition."

Carswell looked at Foster as though weighing how the fellow would take a refusal. Presumably, he read the determination in the other man's eyes because after a moment he bowed clumsily, laughed a trifle shakily, and then said to his new friends, "It seems I must leave you. P'rhaps we'll meet another night. Have to see such marvelous fellows again."

"Certainly, certainly," the two replied suddenly eager to leave him be.

Foster waited until they were out of sight and then said coldly, "Can you walk unsupported, Carswell? Or must I summon transport? For I do not intend to try to carry you myself."

"C'n manage," Carswell said thickly. "Long as I have my cane. See?"

As if to prove it he began to walk, however unsteadily, in the direction of his hotel. Foster joined him, careful to keep a good two feet between them, his lips compressed tightly in patent disapproval of his companion. After several minutes of this, Carswell laughed softly. Foster looked at him sharply and Carswell grinned sheepishly, "Don't like me, do you?" he asked. "Don't blame you. Do wish you'd tell me how you knew who I was."

"I make it my business to know who people are," Foster replied repressively, "particularly when I am informed they have performed a service for someone I am fond of."

"Thought you didn't know your niece very well," Carswell retorted.

"I don't," Foster conceded. "But I know her

family and over the past few days I've had time to form my own opinions of her character. I like Mary and I don't intend to see her hurt."

"Meaning?" Carswell asked with a frown and sounding almost sober.

Foster paused and turned to face Carswell squarely. "Meaning, Captain Carswell, that I do not ever wish to find out that you have presented yourself to see my niece when you are in a condition even remotely resembling your present one. Meaning I also intend to tell her what I have seen tonight."

Carswell's eyes began to twinkle. "But everyone drinks," he protested ingratiatingly.

"Not to this degree, they don't," Foster retorted. "And not in the company of such fellows as I saw you with. I tell you frankly, Carswell, I do not like your taste in friends. Nor to see a man as castaway as you are tonight."

Abruptly, Carswell frowned. "P'rhaps I've more reason to drink than most men," he answered roughly.

"Do you think so?" Foster demanded scathingly. "Why? Because of your leg? Oh, yes, I've heard about that and I can see that it incapacitates you to a degree, but pray forgive me if I refuse to feed your self-pity. Your leg be damned, man! Do you honestly think yourself worse off than all the other wounded who have come home? Particularly the ones who haven't even enough funds to feed themselves, never mind their families? For that matter, never mind the wounded, what about the unwounded men and women, aye and children, who've not got enough to eat or a place to sleep except out in the cold at night. Good God, man, no one led me to think you were such a fool as this!"

Carswell regarded Foster steadily, all amusement gone from his face and voice as he replied, leaning heavily on his cane, "You don't like me, don't approve of me, and yet you patently tried to rescue me from what you obviously regarded as dangerous company. Why, sir?"

"Tried?" Foster exploded. "I damned well succeeded. As for why, I've already told you, haven't I? It's because of my wife and my niece. Gwendolyn is generally not mistaken about people, and she likes you. More than that, however much I may dislike you I cannot deny that you helped my niece when she needed it." He paused, then added heavily, "No doubt you'll dislike me saying this, but I devoutly hope that whatever wellspring of good it was in you that allowed you to help Mary allows you to rescue yourself from whatever this pit is that you've thrown yourself into." A strange look crossed Carswell's face and Foster said roughly, "Oh, to the devil with all this, What you need now is your bed. Come along, we're not far from the Horn and Hare. I'll see you there and p'rhaps everything will look better in the morning. To both of us."

He gently but firmly took Carswell's arm and propelled the fellow forward. It was easier than he expected and he was even more surprised when Carswell said hesitantly, "I'm sorry to have caused you such distress, sir."

Embarrassed, Foster huffed and said, "Oh, well, all young men cause their elders to be distressed far more often than is proper. You're just one more of 'em."

Now the smile lurked again in Carswell's eyes as he said impudently, "And of course, sir, you are so much older."

Foster eyed his companion warily. "I am

delighted the situation amuses you," he retorted caustically. "I only hope you will be just as amused tomorrow morning when you are sober. Now here is your hotel. They will take care of you; I must be on my way." He paused, then added, the hint of steel once more in his voice, "I expect you to present yourself to see me within the week and I expect you to do so sober. And you are not to see my niece again until you have. Is that understood?"

Carswell seemed almost sober already as he replied, steadily, "Yes, of course. I give you my word I shall not do otherwise." He paused, then added, "Thank you for your kindness tonight, sir. And please believe me when I say that I am not always such a ramshackle fellow as I appear to be right now."

"We shall see," Foster replied uncompromisingly. To Carswell's astonishment his eyes began to twinkle as he added, "If you are, I shall have a great deal to say to Gwendolyn on the subject of her judgment of young gentlemen! Good night to you, Carswell, good night."

7

MR. Foster wasted very little time, the next morning over breakfast, in apprising his wife and niece of what he had seen. As was customary, the food had been left in covered dishes on the sideboard and there were no servants hanging about to overhear. "Gwen, my dear, I am afraid Captain Carswell is under orders from me not to try to see Mary until he has my permission, permission that may not be forthcoming."

Unfazed, his wife merely poured Foster more coffee and then said, "Yes, Hubert. I gather he has somehow disgraced himself, then?"

Foster looked at his niece's pale face and shrugged. "No, not qutie as bad as that," he answered with a frown. "But I did find him in deplorable condition last night, with deplorable acquaintances, and until I can discover how frequent such occurrences are, I should merely like to be careful. He is to present himself here, to see me, within the week."

Her gaze steady, Mary addressed her uncle. "I collect you to mean you found Captain Carswell drunk somewhere, last night, and disliked his company. But I can assure you that in the time I spent with him in Ipswich I saw none of that."

"You would not have," Foster replied curtly. "I give the man that much credit. But what he did after you retired for the night you cannot know for certain."

"But the point is that he did not behave so in my company," Mary persisted.

"No, Mary," her Aunt Gwendolyn said gently, "the point is that if Captain Carswell makes a habit of such behavior he will soon put himself beyond the pale of what is acceptable to the *ton* and that will do your credit no good if your name is linked with his."

"Why then mine should be," Mary said bravely. "For if the truth were known, then surely I should already be considered beyond the pale."

Hubert Foster hesitated and, in the end, left it to his wife to tactfully reply. Gwendolyn Foster shook her lovely head and said with a smile, "There is a vast difference, my dear, between your naive actions and the choice a man as seasoned as Captain Carswell makes to drink himself to oblivion. Moreover, if his judgment in friends so easily deserts him when he is four sheets to the wind, then one cannot say in what other ways his judgment will desert him at such a time." She paused, then looked at her husband and said frankly, "Perhaps I was mistaken in urging him to remain in Brighton, after all."

Foster patted her hand reassuringly. "Perhaps not, my dear." His eyes distinctly twinkled as he added, "After all, I cannot believe your judgment is so bad that you would have liked the fellow as much as you did if he were truly a hopeless case.

No doubt he will have a perfectly acceptable explanation when he comes to call and Mary may see him as much as she likes."

Mary, who had by now recovered her composure, replied scathingly, "Or at any rate as often as the captain likes. He has the most appallingly proper notions of propriety, Uncle Hubert."

"Does he indeed?" Foster asked thoughtfully. "Do you know, Gwen, I am becoming quite intrigued with this young man. A pity he is unlikely to be in any condition to present himself here for at least a day or two!"

That assessment was one grimly shared by the fellow who had just entered Carswell's apartments and was now staring down at his sleeping figure.

A moment later Carswell came awake with a start and a curse as a wet cloth was flung over his face. Blinking open his eyes he was confronted by his unsmiling friend Freddy. "What the devil are you doing here?" Carswell managed to ask thickly.

Sitting on the edge of a chair, well out of arm's reach, Freddy said cheerfully, "Come to get you up and out of bed. Not my fault if you had a heavy night of it."

"I should have taken you along and then you'd still be in bed and in no shape to abuse me this way," Carswell muttered in return. "What the devil are you doing here?"

"That's twice you've asked the same question," Freddy replied, still amiably. "Must watch that, old fellow."

"Then answer it!" Carswell all but roared.

"I'm here to have you introduce me to an

heiress, of course," Freddy replied as though there were no other possible answer.

Carswell blinked. "You're an hallucination," he declared. "That's what it must be."

"No, no, coming it much too strong," Freddy said with a laugh. "Nightmare, perhaps, but not an hallucination. Come, what do you find so difficult to believe about my request? Now that I'm the Viscount Halliwell and you know I must marry, and why not an heiress? I'm presentable enough. And since you know one, why not ask you to introduce us?"

"P'rhaps I mean to marry her myself," Carswell said with a grin.

Freddy shook his head. "Impossible. The only way you'll ever be leg-shackled is if it's done by force. B'sides, I have it upon excellent authority—yours—that you are merely an old friend of the family and haven't the least interest in the chit yourself."

"The devil, you say," Carswell said with a frown.

"No, you say it, or rather said it yesterday," Freddy corrected his friend serenely. "Or has that somehow changed since then?"

Carswell glared at his friend, his wits finally beginning to function. "No, that hasn't changed," he concurred reluctantly, "but I still can't introduce you to Miss Farnham."

"Why not?" Freddy persisted.

"Because I find myself in deep disgrace with her uncle," Carswell replied with a frown. "Mr. Foster encountered me upon my way home last night and took exception both to my condition and my company. I am forbidden to see Miss Farnham again until I present myself sober to her uncle and pass inspection and, I suspect, a sharp grilling."

Freddy sucked in his breath, serious for once as he said, "That bad was it? I wondered why you invited none of us to join you. Still fretting about your leg?"

Carswell hesitated, as though debating what to answer. At last he said, "Yes. No. Dammit, what difference does it make whether I am fretting over my leg or over my father and brother? What difference is there to choose between them?"

"Self-pity don't become you," Freddy said frankly.

Carswell rounded on his friend. "Easy for you to say! You're the eldest son and already become the viscount. You've no need to wonder how your bills will be met or if your father will condescend to give you an adequate allowance. No, nor need to face the humiliation of hearing it lasts only so long as you do not show your face on home ground! And as for your health, you can damn well dance the night away without paying for it the next day with agony in your right leg. So don't talk to me of self-pity."

"Do you know, I have the oddest feeling you're not telling me the truth," Freddy said thoughtfully.

Carswell merely turned his back upon his friend and retorted, "You may as well leave, you know. I've already told you I can't do what you wish."

To the captain's chagrin but not surprise, Freddy merely stood, clapped Carswell on the shoulder, and said cheerfully, "Of course you can. You can wash up, dress, have a decent meal with me, and then go straight round to present yourself to Miss Farnham's uncle. I'll even come with you to support your case and as soon as you have retrieved his good opinion of you, you may introduce me to Miss Farnham." Carswell did not at once answer and after a moment Freddy said quietly and soberly, "You may as well, you know. Once the *ton* learns of her existence, provided she does not have a stammer or squint or some such liability, of course, then there will be a great many young men pursuing her. I may as well be one of them. At least you know I am not a fortune hunter."

"Do I?" Carswell asked with a crooked smile. "P'rhaps you've already run through your father's fortune and mean to retrieve yourself with an advantageous marriage."

Having earned himself the sobriquet of "sad sobriety" while in the Hussars with Carswell, Langley, and Jack, Freddy could laugh and retort, "Now, now, you weren't to learn that until *after* the knot was tied!" Then, more quietly, he asked, "Come, will you do it? Or do you mean to have a touch at her yourself after all?"

"Me?" Carswell asked with mock disbelief. "Scarcely, my friend. I've no wish to figure as one of those fortune hunters you just spoke of." He paused and shook his head. "Give me half an hour and order us up some food, and then we shall see. If I can make myself presentable we shall then go round and make my apologies to Mr. Foster."

"Excellent!" his friend told him approvingly. "I knew you would come to your senses, sooner or later. After all, it is to your advantage to have friends who have deep pockets, you know."

8

LADY Crane and her daughter, Desmona, were visiting the Foster household when Captain Carswell and the viscount arrived. Since the gentlemen had requested to speak with Mr. Foster, however, the ladies were not apprised of their arrival. Instead, Desmona and Mary quickly became engaged in a comparison of fashions and other girlish topics while the two elder ladies exchanged the latest *on-dits* and made plans for Mary's introduction to those members of the *ton* who had made Brighton their home for the summer.

"If only Prinny may decide to come, you are assured of invitations for Mr. Foster, yourself, and Mary," Lady Crane said with a sigh. "And however much they may talk about him, very few would refuse to follow his lead in inviting your niece out and about."

"Perhaps he will yet come, although I do not depend upon it," Gwendolyn Foster said with a smile. "If nothing else develops, I shall give a small card party and introduce Mary there. One glimpse of the girl and word will soon spread that there is a new beauty to be seen."

For a moment both ladies regarded Miss
Farnham and then Lady Crane said hesitantly, "To
be sure, she is a beauty, but might it not help to
also let it be known she is an heiress?"

Gwendolyn shook her head decisively. "I've no
wish to have my niece pursued for her money. In
any event, it will be some time before she can
touch the funds and therefore the argument loses
some of its cogency as a motive for marriage. I
should not wish any suitor to later feel deceived,
after the wedding."

"Sensible of you," Lady Crane said with a thin
smile. Then, avoiding her hostess's eyes she said,
"By the by, does that, er, Captain Caldwell remain
in Brighton long?"

Mrs. Foster was not deceived by her friend's
careless tones. Coolly she replied, "Captain
Carswell remains for as long as he chooses, I
imagine, although he has not, of course, confided
in us his plans."

"A pity he is a younger son," Lady Crane said
affably. "And a cripple into the bargain."

Both ladies smiled at one another, grim under-
standing hidden behind faces of amiability.

Meanwhile, Mr. Hubert Foster regarded his two
visitors with great care. The walls of the book
room were lined with volumes collected over the
past twenty years and Viscount Halliwell seemed
to find them of great interest. As for Captain
Carswell, the bright afternoon sun streaming
through the sheer curtains at the windows was not
flattering to his face. He looked as though he
required a few more hours of sleep and some
kindness to banish the lines of bleakness that
seemed to have become habitual to him. Hubert

Foster found some of his anger fading in the face of the man's evident distress. Captain Carswell had said little beyond greeting Foster conventionally and introducing the viscount, but already Foster found himself liking the fellow in spite of his determination to be coldly rational about the business.

It was with an effort that Foster was able to say harshly, "I should like to know, Carswell, how frequently you indulge in the sort of behavior I saw last night?"

The captain glanced at his friend but Freddy was pretending a great interest in one of Mr. Foster's volumes of Shakespeare and Carswell could not catch his eye. Soberly, he looked at Hubert and said, quietly, "I have known many young men to do far worse."

"Yes, callow boys!" Foster exploded with anger. "But you are not a callow boy, you are nine and twenty years of age and, one would have thought past such things. The only times I have known men who indulged in such behavior at your age, they were headed rapidly either to an early grave or to an unenviable reputation that must make them anathema to any respectable person."

"Particularly any respectable person with a marriageable girl about," Carswell suggested with heavy irony.

Foster's color rose and Halliwell hastily intervened, "Mr. Foster, I assure you that it is no such thing with Randall. If, from time to time, the difficulties of his situation cause him to behave a trifle foolishly, I assure you it is not an everyday occurrence!"

Mr. Foster rose from the desk he was sitting behind and began to pace the room. He did not look at his guests as he spoke. "I am aware, Captain Carswell, of the evils of your situation and believe me when I say that I feel for you. But I am also too well aware of the temptation that must exist to drown the realities that face you with the strong libations offered at this town's taverns. Too great a temptation, perhaps. I should like nothing better than for you to befriend my niece, since it is apparent to me that she benefits greatly from your good sense. Good sense you appear unable to apply to yourself."

Foster swung around and faced Carswell squarely. They were, Randall realized with a pang of surprise, of much the same height, and all trace of fatuity disappeared as the man met his eyes, the challenge aparent in them as Hubert Foster said, "I shall have to ask you, therefore, if you can say to me, Captain Carswell, that the scene I saw last night will not be repeated while you are in Brighton." Carswell hesitated and Foster added, with patent frustration, "Damn you, man, surely you see that those fellows you were with only wished to take advantage of you? Surely you cannot wish to see them again?"

It was Carswell's turn to look away. As he limped to the window and stared out of it, the Viscount Halliwell and Mr. Foster watched him with astonishment. "Is it so difficult to make such a pledge, then, Captain Carswell?" Foster asked incredulously.

"Randall? Are matters truly come to such a terrible pass?" Freddy asked, concern filling his quiet voice which no longer held its accustomed levity.

For the first time Carswell felt fully the evils of his position. A hint of desperation in his eyes, he turned to the two men and said, "Can you not believe that what you saw, Mr. Foster, was not as terrible as it seemed?"

With a level gaze Hubert replied, "You forget, Captain Carswell, that I have some knowledge of who those men may be. They are not harmless fellows." He paused and said coaxingly, "Come, can you not promise to avoid them? I do not ask sobriety of you, merely that you show more discretion in your choice of drinking companions. And that when you wish to drink you do so with a trifle more moderation. Is that so difficult a pledge to make?"

"Yes," Carswell replied curtly.

"Then I must tell you that until such a time as you can give me the assurances I have asked for, I must warn you not to call upon my niece," Foster said quietly, his jaw set with determination.

For a long, appalled moment no one spoke. Then Carswell said, his voice a trifle unsteady, "I regret, Mr. Foster, that I am not in a position to leave Brighton immediately. I had intended to do so yesterday, but circumstances now compel me to remain. I am sure you will understand that if I cannot give you the first pledge you asked for that I will also not give you the second." He smiled charmingly but almost seemed to sway upon his feet as he turned to Freddy and said with an apologetic air, "I'm sorry, old friend. I hope I have not given Mr. Foster a dislike of you into the bargain. And I have no doubt that I have disappointed you as well. If you choose to cut me I shall quite understand."

"Don't be a fool, man!" Freddy retorted, clapping his friend upon the shoulder.

Carswell shrugged away the hand as he turned

to Hubert and said, "Before I take my leave, I beg,
Mr. Foster, that you will not allow your poor
opinion of me to carry over to Lord Halliwell. If
you ask about, you will discover that his reputation, unlike mine, is beyond reproach. Indeed, we
were used to call him 'sad sobriety' in jest when
we all wore colors. I brought him here today
meaning to introduce him to your niece. I beg you
will still do so, as I assure you that whatever faults
I possess, he does not share them. Good day, Mr.
Foster. Freddy, good-bye."

With that astonishing abruptness, Carswell
walked out of the room before either man could
sufficiently recover to stop him. Halliwell would
have followed but Foster stopped him by placing a
hand on his arm. "A moment, if you please, Lord
Halliwell. You cannot help your friend by rushing
after him, but perhaps you can help him by
staying and answering some questions I still have
about Captain Carswell. And then, if you wish, I
shall indeed introduce you to my niece."

His jaw set Freddy replied evenly, "I shall stay,
since you believe that in doing so I may serve my
friend Carswell. But at the moment I assure you
that meeting your niece is not of the highest
priority in my mind, however eager you may be to
provide her with another suitor."

To his surprise, Foster laughed. "Please sit
down, Lord Halliwell. I assure you I am not in the
least impatient to have Mary off my hands and I
should have thought less of you if you had jumped
at my offer to meet her. But I do wish you will tell
me more about yourself and about Captain
Carswell. I have never liked so well a man I was so
forced to disapprove and I should like some under-
standing of why this should be so. Perhaps you can
help me and we can both help him."

The Viscount Halliwell stayed.

By common consent neither Hubert Foster nor the Viscount Halliwell, when he was presented to Miss Farnham, told Mary what had occurred. Halliwell was presented as an acquaintance of an acquaintance and nothing more. He stayed the proper half hour, dividing his attention equally between the two elder women and the two younger, before he took his leave. Shortly after that, Lady Crane and her daughter bore Mary off to Donaldson's library to introduce her to that admirable social edifice. Noting the preoccupied look upon her spouse's face, Gwendolyn declined to accompany them.

When Mary had been safely seen off, dressed in a walking gown of sea blue and matching parasol, Gwendolyn turned to her husband and said, "Well, will you tell me what has occurred to distress you, Hubert? And precisely whose acquaintance is Lord Halliwell?"

Foster hesitated a moment before answering. "How are you feeling, my love?" he prevaricated. "Past being distressed in the mornings? What does the accoucheur say?"

"That having a baby is a perfectly natural occurrence, as you very well know, Hubert," she retorted amiably.

"Your mother had difficulties," Foster countered irritably. "There was nothing natural about the process for her."

"That is why Sir Geoffrey Botham has already said that should the child appear too large for my bones he will bring me to bed a good month early," Gwendolyn replied placidly. "You know he did so with Lady Botham. She told me that with care the child is at no greater risk than if I went the full course. Less, in fact, since there need not be the danger of losing the child to save me." She paused, then took his hand and said, "But come, Hubert, tell me what is troubling you, for I know it is not this. We have discussed it all before and both want very much for this child to be born. Is it Mary?" she hazarded shrewdly.

Reluctantly he nodded. It had never been his habit to hide what he knew from Gwendolyn and he found he could not begin now. He told her what had transpired in his meeting with Carswell and what Halliwell had added after the captain departed the house. When he was done Gwendolyn drew a deep breath. "Well," she said, "at any rate, I cannot believe he is likely to try to approach Mary. He was reluctant enough to call upon her just two days ago because of the fact of her being an heiress. I was half tempted to tell him our suspicions concerning her stepfather and her inheritance. But I did not. I wonder what changed Captain Carswell's mind about staying in Brighton?"

"I can only hope it was the discovery that his old friends were here, not the acquiring of those new ones that did it," Hubert said with distaste.

"Are they so very bad, then," Mary asked hesitantly.

Hubert nodded. "Do you recall the trouble this past winter with the refugees come over from France? Sheer riffraff, some of them. Well, the two I saw with Carswell last night rank among the worst of the mischief makers. No, I could not overlook the captain's taking up with such men. But I am concerned about Mary. What shall we tell her?"

Gwendolyn spoke with great reluctance. "I can

not help but almost wish he would break your ban concerning Mary." At Hubert's look of astonishment and outrage she smiled and said, "Peace, love, I know very well it would not do, but he did have the knack of handling her when she took up these nonsensical notions about the theater. As for what we shall tell Mary, the answer is nothing until she asks. Which will not, I think, be for some few days. Perhaps by then the viscount or some other gentleman shall have found a place in her affections and she will take the news with less distress. Perhaps we should go ahead and plan that card party right away."

Hubert Foster nodded. "I quite agree. But do leave two weeks from today free, for I expect we shall be dining at the Marine Pavilion then."

"Prinny is in town?" Gwendolyn asked. "I had not heard so."

"He is not but as he has made a wager that he shall make the journey in under four hours, ten days from now, I think we may believe that the informal note I have received from Prinny's secretary will soon be followed by a proper invitation." He paused and said meditatively, "I should think that the knowledge that one was to dine with the Prince Regent of England would exercise a great portion of the imagination of a young lady so favored."

Gwendolyn laughed. "And so it shall. I shall have Mary's mind all in a whirl with the thought of what gown to wear, and with choosing fabrics and trims and fittings and such I should be much surprised if the girl had time to mope."

Hubert moved closer to his wife. Tracing the curve of her face and neck with one finger he said, thoughtfully, "And to think anyone ever wondered why I should have wished to marry you! What fools mere mortals may be."

Without a word Gwendolyn rose and, her eyes dancing with unspoken laughter, she led the way upstairs, much to the scandal of the upper housemaid who later confided in awed tones to the footman that it had not even been three of the afternoon clock when the couple shut the bedroom door behind them!

9

IT was not to be expected that Mary Farnham would fail to notice Captain Carswell's desertion. Nor did it require more than one evasive answer from her aunt for her to acquire a tolerably accurate notion of what had transpired. Another young lady might have given way to tears or stormed and railed at her guardians. Or, though it seems unlikely, meekly accepted the state of affairs.

Mary Farnham, however, was neither a milk and water chit nor a fool. Although her age was only nineteen, the years of living in a hostile household had matured her far beyond that, for even before her mother's remarriage Mary had never been a favored daughter.

To be sure, in matters of the heart Mary Farnham was an innocent. For his own reasons her stepfather had never consented to a Season for Mary or even a local come-out. But that scarcely mattered now. Mary was accustomed to acting without advice from anyone and to doing what must be done. Therefore, what occurred when she realized the full import of Carswell's disappearance was in character for her. She did not wish to distress her aunt by indulging in outrageous behavior and she had, moreover, too much pride to like the notion of throwing herself at Captain Carswell's head. So it took some time to make up her mind. Until the night of Prinny's dinner party, in fact.

Miss Farnham had, by then, seen the captain frequently around and about Brighton and he had given her no more than the coolest of bows. As for conversation, he strictly refused it and not once did his knock sound at their door. Naturally, he did not appear at the card party given by Mrs. Foster in Mary's honor that was accounted such a social success.

As Gwendolyn had predicted, the news that they were to dine at the Marine Pavilion with the Prince of Wales, Regent of England, had exercised a powerful effect upon Mary. She had been as anxious as her aunt to acquire a new dress and the correct gloves and slippers to accompany it. Fortunately, Mrs. Foster's favorite modiste was quick as well as fashionable and was able to provide Mary with a completed gown by the evening of the Regent's dinner party.

"Your dress ought, of course, to be white," Gwendolyn acknowledged as she watched her maid put the finishing touches on Mary's coiffure, "but white can scarcely be said to be your best color. In any event, since you are nineteen I think we may escape the strictures laid at the door of a chit just leaving the schoolroom. This suits you far better."

Mary fingered the trim of her dress made of green lace over green satin. "Yes, but I am just now making my come-out," she said, without great conviction.

"That is precisely what I will not accept," Gwendolyn said bluntly. "Whatever reason made your mother so absurd as to neglect her responsibilities to a daughter, the fault cannot be laid at your door. No one here need know that this is your first major party. Depend upon it, everyone will assume that you simply had a quiet come-out in the country and will not question the matter. If they do you need not lie, merely say that family considerations made it impossible for you to be presented sooner. Which is quite true. No one will press you further." She paused and looked at her niece with a critical eye. Then, with a sigh she said, "A thousand pities you are too young to wear emeralds for they would be perfect with that dress. But there is no sense in being foolish. In any event, those pearls look delightful on you."

Rather shyly Mary said, "You have been so kind to me that I can scarcely credit it! All these clothes, the pearls, everything. And at such a time as this for me to intrude upon you!"

With a haughtiness that was belied by the twinkle in her eyes, Gwendolyn drew herself to her full height and said, "At such a time as what?"

"Your . . . your condition," Mary stammered.

Gwendolyn looked down with satisfaction at the outfit she wore. It was of rose satin and lace with rubies at her ears and throat, and matching gloves and slippers to complete the outfit which proclaimed her one of the most attractive ladies in Brighton. "What condition?" she asked coolly. "I didn't think I looked ill."

Impulsively, Mary took her aunt's hands. "Of course you don't look ill," she said. "Indeed, I have never seen anyone look so delightful when they were breeding. But I cannot help thinking I must be a nuisance at a time like this. My mama always said I was. She also said that breeding was one of the worst fates that could befall a woman."

A frown replaced the twinkle in Gwendolyn's eyes as she replied seriously, "My dear, you could never be a nuisance. As for breeding being an evil, it is only if one thinks it so or if society deems it so. But for me, I have found it a delight in spite of everything. Though to be sure it is not that long since I have known." She paused to glance in the mirror, then said complacently, "How fortunate for me that the style is not to be laced tightly in. With this dress I should be much surprised if anyone can even guess. Now come. Let us go find your uncle, who is no doubt pacing back and forth and impatiently looking at his timepiece while he waits for us. Besides, it is almost six o'clock and whatever else one may be late for, dinner with the Prince of Wales does not allow for tardiness."

A short time later they were entering the Pavilion. Mary had passed by it before, of course. One could not be in Brighton and not do so. But it still seemed to her a trifle overwhelming, with its domes and columns and Indian, Moslem, and Chinese elements. Nor was the interior less extravagant. Mary only had time to ask a whispered question of her aunt before they were shown into the domed drawing room with the other guests. "Who serves as the Regent's hostess?" she said.

Hastily, Gwendolyn whispered her own reply, "He has none. When we go in to dinner he will escort whomever is the highest ranking lady."

Many of the other guests had already arrived and Mrs. Foster and her husband introduced Mary to those acquaintances she had not yet met. Then, shortly before six-thirty, when the Prince of Wales was due to arrive, the Viscount Halliwell, Captain Carswell, and two other gentlemen were shown in. The former bowed and nodded in a friendly way in the direction of the Fosters, but Carswell, after one careless glance and a rigidly polite bow, resolutely turned his back upon them.

Mary would have gone toward him, in spite of everything, but just then Prinny entered the room and Gwendolyn and Mary, along with the other ladies, immediately rose. The girl stared at the man who had been a part of the gossip she had overheard all of her life. He looked neither the wild libertine nor the power-hungry tyrant nor the handsome princeling she had heard described. Instead, the Prince of Wales seemed to her a kindly, courteous, middle-aged, rather corpulent man who tried to put his guests at ease. Mary could not see that he overlooked anyone, even herself, in greeting his guests. "Good evening, Foster, Mrs. Foster," he said affably when it was their turn. "Who is this lovely young lady?"

"My niece, Miss Mary Farnham, come from the country to stay with us a while," Hubert said calmly.

Mary made a deep curtsy and found herself looking up into eyes that twinkled with amusement. "Well, my dear, I'm not half the ogre you've no doubt heard me painted, am I? How do you like Brighton?"

"I find it a lovely place," Mary answered judiciously, "though I cannot help but wonder if it is not a trifle cold in winter."

Prinny seemed genuinely pleased by her reply. "Precisely!" he said at once. "And yet I like the place so well I cannot keep away. That is why I have gone to such trouble to see that we have the most excellent of heating systems in the Pavilion. Central heating from a patent stove. Had you noticed?"

Avoiding the Regent's eyes, Mary swallowed and permitted herself to say meekly, "Why, yes, I had noticed the heating. It is extraordinary."

"Capital, capital!" the Prince of Wales said, rubbing his hands together. "There is nothing to equal it. Well, you must excuse me now, I must say hello to Lady Crane."

When he was out of earshot Mary turned to her aunt and asked in disbelief, "Is he really proud of the temperature in here? I am suffocating."

Gwendolyn looked about at all of the guests surreptitiously fanning themselves, and nodded. In a voice that betrayed nothing she said, "The Regent is subject to chills."

"Not quite what you expected, is it?" Hubert Foster asked amiably.

Mary looked around slowly. "No, no, it is not. In Essex we had heard rumors—"

She broke off in confusion and Hubert went on, gently, "In Essex, no doubt you heard rumors of wild debaucheries here at the Marine Pavilion. Scarcely short of orgies, I don't doubt. Well, you can see for yourself that the delicate furnishings would not allow for much of that. And I fear, my dear, that rather than finding yourself shocked you are far more likely to find the proceedings dreadfully staid and proper tonight. Unless, of course, Prinny should call for his air guns and take to firing them over the dinner table again, but he has not done that for some time." He paused and looked at the back of the Regent, across the room from them now, and went on, "Do you know, I have often thought that Prinny wanted to be a good ruler and that his worst excesses are a rebellion against the turkish treatment he received as a child."

Gwendolyn tapped her husband's arm reprovingly with her fan and said, "Nonsense, Hubert. The man is as he is and there is no sense in wondering the reasons. Suffice it to say, Mary, that however absurd a figure he may sometimes appear, the Prince also has moments of great kindness and worthiness."

"Which is why you are in the process of cutting his character to shreds?" a voice asked with unbridled sarcasm from behind them.

Gwendolyn Foster turned and looked at the newcomer with a cool gaze as she replied, "I have never thought, Captain Carswell, that friendship or even admiration required that one turn a blind eye upon the faults of others. I should not like the Prince of Wales half so well if he were not so evidently human."

Carswell bowed with great irony, prompting a snort from Hubert Foster. Immediately the captain addressed him. "Yes, yes, I know you wish me at Jericho. But I only wish to introduce to you two more of my friends. I understand that you have been kind enough to allow Halliwell to call and I thought you might be equally generous with my good friends Major Langley and Captain Wollcott."

Irritably, Hubert said, "You might have done better to have let Halliwell recommend them."

Carswell lifted his eyebrows in apparent disbelief. "And have everyone here wonder why, when I am such an old friend of the family, I must ask someone else to introduce my friends to you?"

"Very well," Foster said curtly, "bring them over."

"I shall be back in a trice."

Captain Carswell moved away without so much as a glance at Mary Farnham's rigidly polite face. He did not need to look at it, he thought with a smile, to guess what her thoughts held.

Before the introductions could be completed, however, dinner was announced and the party moved from the drawing room with its domed ceiling to the dining room with its ceiling painted like the evening sky, a very long dining table, a fanciful chandelier, and dinner music in the background. To her astonishment, Mary found herself placed next to Captain Carswell, a circumstance that caused her generally amiable aunt to purse her lips in patent disapproval. On Mary's other side was Major Langley.

"Not precisely according to etiquette," that gentleman confided to Miss Farnham under cover of the confusion of everyone finding their place cards, "but Prinny has a fondness for Carswell. No doubt he thought the pair of you would be pleased to be placed together."

"Oh, I assure you, I am pleased," Mary replied with vehemence, "however Captain Carswell may feel about the matter."

But Carswell did not appear equally pleased. Every time Mary turned to him in an attempt to engage him in conversation she discovered him conversing with the women who sat on his other side. Thus Mary was thrown into the company of Major Langley, who exerted himself to amuse her. As her eyes widened at the profusion of dishes he told her softly, "Have a care to your appetite. It is not unusual for the covers to number in the dozens with thirty-six reserved for the entrees alone. Which no doubt is one reason the Prince of Wales has acquired such a generous figure."

"You appear very familiar with the customs that obtain here," Mary hazarded, "Are you also a particular friend of the Prince Regent?"

Langley shook his head and gave a lazy laugh, "Not friend, precisely. My father was a friend of his when they were both young, as were Carswell's father, Lord Atley, the late Viscount Halliwell, and Jack Wollcott's father. And they were all friends of each other. I suppose that's one reason why we all ended up together buying our colors and going to war with Wellington."

With a puzzled frown Mary said, "Have you all sold out, then?"

Langley shook his head. "Halliwell and Carswell did. But Jack and I are still officially members of Wellington's staff. On leave, at present."

"That's odd," Mary said without thinking. "I should have thought that matters in Europe would require the attention of all possible officers."

Langley shifted in his chair uneasily but his voice was light as he replied, "Oh, every now and again the Duke of Wellington becomes devilish tired of the lot of us and sends us off, one or two at a time, to England to rest a bit before we return to the fray."

"Of course," Mary retorted coolly, "I can see how he would easily grow tired of someone like Captain Carswell, but I cannot allow that you are equally as provoking."

"Ah, but that is simply because you don't know me well enough. I assure you I can be terribly provoking," Langley retorted archly. Then, to her horror, he spoke across her to the captain and said, "Isn't that so, Carswell?"

Captain Carswell turned and regarded the pair of them with raised eyebrows. "Isn't what so?" he asked in a rigidly polite voice.

"Why, that I can be just as provoking as you," Langley explained with a grin.

Mary Farnham colored deeply and tried to evade Carswell's eyes. She could not evade, however, his voice as he replied curtly, "Neither of us can hold a candle to Miss Farnham, I assure you."

Now her temper was aroused and, with her eyes flashing angrily, Mary retorted, "That's not fair! You know very well the circumstances that led to what occurred. And I did listen to reason when you explained the situation to me. Or do you think I should have accepted unquestioningly everything you said?"

"Miss Farnham," Carswell said coolly, "I never look for miracles."

"You are undoubtedly the most provoking man I have ever met!" Mary told him in a furious whisper.

"No doubt," Carswell agreed amiably. "However, at the moment you are also making me one of the most notorious. Do you think that if you tried you could keep from making us the center of all eyes?"

With an effort Miss Farnham composed herself and said with a false smile and cordial voice, "Why certainly, Captain Carswell. Do let us talk of other matters. When do we see you again at my aunt's house?"

Under the table Mary felt a heavy foot trod on hers. She could not doubt it was Carswell's. "I really cannot say," he replied. Under his breath, however, he added, "In time, Miss Farnham, I shall tell you everything. You have far too much sense to regard the illusion as the reality." He gave her an encouraging smile and then turned back to his other dinner partner.

Unwilling to make herself even more a subject for gossip Mary turned back to Langley and began to talk amiably with him about Brighton. Her determination to beard Carswell, however, had just been fixed. She even began to plan the means of doing so, growing further incensed as Captain Carswell avoided her company for the rest of the evening. Indeed, one might have said that the carefully planned musical entertainment was entirely lost on Miss Farnham.

10

SOMEHOW the evening ended and the guests returned to their respective lodgings. Mary was unexpectedly subdued and the Fosters correctly attributed it to the coldness of Captain Carswell's behavior toward her. They were sorry for her unhappiness but pleased that the captain had sufficient delicacy of feeling to obey their request that he not speak with Miss Farnham but also not tell her why. It was a pity for them that they were not sufficiently acquainted with Mary yet to realize how ominous her meekness might be. On the other hand, since they could not have prevented what was about to occur, perhaps it was just as well that they had no forewarning. At least for two more nights the Fosters were able to sleep peacefully. Indeed, with the off-handed way Mary dismissed the entire evening, they mistakenly congratulated themselves upon their handling of the matter.

The next morning, as had become habitual, a number of young gentlemen came to call upon the Fosters and beg the favor of taking Miss Farnham for a walk or drive. The Viscount Halliwell was among them and although she had not, heretofore, singled him out, she now accepted his offer of a morning drive. He was very pleased and even took in good part the mock anger of his rivals. Nor was he in the least impatient as Mary went upstairs to change to a walking dress of blue jaconet muslin.

The day was a fine, sunny one and Halliwell a neat hand with his horses. Nevertheless, Mary waited until they had left the streets of Brighton behind for the countryside before she abandoned the pleasantries they had been exchanging and began her quest for the information she required.

In a deceptively careless tone she said, "I have not seen Captain Carswell about much. Is he still staying at the Horn and Hare?"

"Yes, he is," Halliwell replied. "I think he finds the air in Brighton bracing."

Mary nodded. "How pleasant for him," she said coolly. "A pity it has not improved his manners. You must know he has not even had the courtesy to call upon us once in the past two weeks. But then, perhaps I should count myself fortunate for that."

Halliwell could not help but feel a small annoyance at Miss Farnham's cavalier dismissal of his friend. His conscience persisted in reminding him that Randall's desertion of Miss Farnham was not by his own choice. A trifle abruptly he asked, "Why did you want to know where Carswell is staying?"

"So that I may avoid encountering the captain, of course," Mary retorted tartly. "I should like to spare us both the embarrassment of meeting in the street outside his lodgings and I feared he might have taken such near my aunt and uncle's house, as I understand certain other young gentlemen have done, of late." Noting that Halliwell still did not appear entirely convinced, Mary changed the subject, almost purring with her voice as she said, "But tell me, Lord Halliwell, how was it to be a soldier in the Peninsula? I have it upon excellent authority that you were a hero!"

Now the Viscount Halliwell was not an egotistical man but neither was he so inhuman as to be impervious to the lure of Mary's upturned eyes regarding him with patent admiration. A trifle self-consciously he said, "Well, er, Miss Farnham, either we were all heroes or none of us. It wasn't a glamorous time or an easy one. Not for officers nor for the men under us. Cold, discomfort, death, and pain were our constant companions. Never let anyone tell you that war is a glorious thing, Miss Farnham. Neither killing nor wishing to kill the enemy makes a man a hero. It is rather the ability to rise above the daily discomforts and frustrations and fear that are all part and parcel of war that separates those who will become heroes from those who merely endure. And in the end one comes away knowing that although there are times when one feels one must fight to preserve that which is important, there is never a time when sane men long for war."

He paused with a distant look in his eyes, then went on, "We killed boys, Miss Farnham, far more often than we killed men, though I doubt they saw themselves as such. Boys and men with much the same hopes and dreams and needs as we ourselves had, following orders that often were little different than our own. I could not help but think, sometimes, that had I been born a peasant in France I, too, would have found myself fighting on their side and dying for a cause I would have thought was just. We have to fight Napoleon, Miss Farnham, but not with joy, only with determination."

Mary had no answer to that and, after a moment, Halliwell said, a trifle sheepishly, "Forgive me, Miss Farnham. You wished to hear about heroes and I'm afraid I gave a speech."

She shook her head. "Don't be sorry. I was just thinking, however, that your views seem remarkably similar to Captain Carswell's."

Halliwell coughed. "Yes, well, we all thought highly of Randall. He used to speak of how he felt about the war and one found it impossible to disagree with him. He had a knack of putting his finger precisely on what was happening and seeing it without the trappings of glory." He noticed her pale face and asked with some concern, "Are you all right, Miss Farnham? I hope I have not distressed you with this blunt talk of war. It really isn't a fit subject for ladies."

She shook her head. "No. I am grateful to you. And to Captain Carswell. No one else has had the courage or perhaps the knowledge to speak frankly to me about the war. It is difficult for those of us who have never seen battle to imagine what it must be like. But I think I should prefer the truth to some pretty fairy tale."

"Now, Miss Farnham," Halliwell said warmly, "I understand why Randall spoke so highly of you!"

The rest of the drive was accomplished in much good humor and Mary Farnham was well pleased when Halliwell returned her to her door. Gwendolyn Foster was just as pleased to see the cheerful smile on her niece's face. It was one more reassurance that the girl had recovered from her disappointment in Captain Carswell.

Gwendolyn Foster would not have been so happy, however, if she had known the plan Mary was hatching. Always ready to display a concern about the problems of the servants, Mary paid a short call that afternoon on the young footman who was suffering from a severe toothache. When she had first arrived in the Foster household she had left with him certain articles of clothing, wrapped in a paper parcel, that were not proper for a young lady to have in her own drawers or closet. The footman, somewhat in awe of his mistress's lovely house guest had, without question, stored them for Miss Farnham. Now he produced them without a word, basking in her kind inquiries concerning his tooth.

The clothes were still exactly as Mary had wrapped them up before leaving home. A circumstance she noted with satisfaction. Even if he later wished to, the boy would not be able to tell her Aunt Gwendolyn just what it was she carried away with her that day. Fortunately, she was able to gain her room unseen by any of the other servants or her aunt and uncle.

In the privacy of her room, Mary rang for a tray to be brought with a light luncheon, then dismissed her aunt's maid with the explanation that she wished to rest. This request was conveyed with just the right amount of melancholy to allow the girl to suppose she wished to nurse in secret a developing *tendre*. As soon as the girl had delivered the tray and was gone, Mary drew out from under her bed the parcel and undid the strings.

A few minutes later she was dressed in her stepbrother Thomas's clothing, looking very much like a young man about town. She could not, of course, have passed close scrutiny in daylight. The sunlight would have revealed too clearly her curves and girlish features to probing eyes as well as the abundant hair upon her head. At night, however, with her hair brushed neatly back and tied at the neck in an oldfashioned way, as well as with the protection afforded by a hat, she might pass as a rather provincial young gentleman. And it would certainly be safer, Mary told herself, to go out alone dressed as a young man than as a young woman, particularly in the parts of town she feared she might have to visit.

Mary had stolen the clothes out of her stepbrother's room some months ago when she first determined to run away. With her breasts confined by a long strip of cloth wound round her chest several times and her hair forced smooth and bound at the neck, Mary had felt she might pass muster. Then for hours at a time she had practiced in her room in front of a long looking glass trying to imitate her brother's sharp, masculine walk, careless drawl, and ready frown until she was finally satisfied that she had perfected her portrayal of a young gentleman. She had intended to travel as a woman. But if that had become unsafe she would have tried to pass as a boy. Mary had meant to be prepared for anything.

After trying on the clothes and determining that no rips or tears had occurred in the interval since she had last worn them and that they still fit as well as ever, Mary removed them and hid them once more under the bed. Then, dressed in her own gown she ate the luncheon set for her and went downstairs to while away the afternoon in innocent pursuits that must serve to allay any suspicions her Aunt Gwendolyn might have that she was not entirely happy with her lot.

11

GWENDOLYN and Hubert Foster left for a small dinner party with friends early in the evening. They were a trifle disappointed to hear that Mary had the headache and could not accompany them, but they were not entirely surprised. Once her aunt and uncle had gone, Mary retreated to her room with a cup of the cook's own special posset for headaches and asked the maid to have some bath water brought up and then to lay out her night clothes. Mary was determined to take no chances and the thought that someone might unmask her by the scent she habitually wore, one not usually to be found on a young gentleman, unnerved her. She was determined not to overlook a thing.

Somewhat more than an hour later she stood dressed in her stepbrother's clothes. The bathing tub had been removed some time since and she had been left alone, presumably to seek her bed at an astonishingly early hour. Instead, she prepared to make her way out of the house. Darkness had already fallen and therefore she had only to reach the door and leave by it unseen to be safe. There were too many servants about, however, and in the end she climbed down by the garden trellis that went past her window, having spent much time, over the years, climbing imaginary battlements with her stepbrothers.

For once, Mary thought grimly, there was no one to tell her she had done it all wrong and that she had been killed by the enemy. Her only worry was that a curious neighbor would see her and set it about that young gentlemen were climbing in and out of Miss Farnham's bedroom window. But as that thought did not occur to her until she had all but reached the ground anyway, there was nothing for it but to continue on her way.

Captain Carswell, meanwhile, had been unable to rid himself of his friends Langley, Halliwell, and Wollcott. All three had been determined to carry him off to dinner with them and then to play cards and generally make a night of it together. That was why when Miss Farnham strode into the Horn and Hare she was informed that the captain had gone out, the clerk had no idea when he would return, and no, the young gentleman could not wait in his rooms. Mary declined hastily the offer to wait in the lobby of the inn for she was afraid that the illumination was too bright to sustain her disguise. Instead, she took up a post across the street, standing in the dark and waiting.

Fortunately for her, Carswell had publicly pleaded an ache in his leg and begged to be excused to return to his hotel. His three friends had insisted on escorting him but left the hotel a few minutes later. Mary was still debating whether to call upon him in his room or wait for him to come out again when suddenly two hands closed around her neck. "May I ask why you are so interested in Captain Carswell's whereabouts?" a voice hissed in her ear.

Struggling to keep from blacking out as the grip about her neck tightened, Mary managed to whisper, "He is an acquaintance of my family. I was told to seek him out."

At once the grip slackened and then released her. Rubbing the places where she was sure she would have bruises in the morning, Mary turned to face her assailant. It was a grim-faced Major Langley who regarded her with an unflinching gaze. "Indeed?" he drawled. "And when did you arrive in Brighton, my little stripling?"

"This evening," Mary said in character as a sulky youth. "And I don't see what business it is of yours."

"It is my business because I choose to make it my business," Langley replied, in the same silky voice. His eyes narrowed and he added abruptly, "You look very familiar, boy. Where do I know you from?"

"You don't," Mary retorted.

Langley shrugged and said grimly, "As you wish. It is of no consequence since I am certain to recall the answer soon enough on my own. But tell me, if you are so eager to see Captain Carswell, then why haven't you gone inside and called upon him?"

"I tried," Mary sniffed disdainfully, "but I was told he was out and since the clerk didn't much seem to like me, I figured I'd rather wait outside. Then the cap'n came back, but he had some friends with him and I decided to wait until they left."

"Why?" Langley persisted, still silkily.

"Why?" Mary stalled, hunting for an answer.

"Be—because I thought he wouldn't want his friends to see me."

"Why not?" Langley asked reasonably.

"Be—because I'm an illegitimate cousin," was the answer that burst out of Mary's mouth before she had a chance to think it through.

"His illegitimate cousin?" Langley repeated blankly.

"Yes. And he's been pointed out to me, even though he doesn't know about me yet," Mary embroidered hastily.

"What do you want with him?" Langley asked with a frown. "To cause trouble?"

"No sir," Mary replied with genuine shock. "I just needed to see him."

"Very well, then, let's go see him," Langley said, abruptly coming to a decision. "I'll take you up to his rooms."

That was no part of Mary's plan, but she did not object. How could she? Langley had let go of her neck but with his last words taken firm hold of her arm and begun to drag her across the street to the Horn and Hare. So she went with him without protest. Once she was in Captain Carswell's rooms she would have to think of some way to handle matters better.

As for Carswell, he was not pleased to hear the knock at his parlor door and Langley's bluff voice call out, "Randall! Open up. I've a cousin of yours with me, or so he says."

"What the devil?" Carswell's exclamation as he opened the door was cut short by the sight of his supposed cousin. With narrowed eyes his gaze raked over the youth Langley held by the arm and after a moment he said evenly, "I think you had best come in.

"So you are my cousin?" he asked the youth

skeptically. "By my mother's side or by my father's? And where on earth did you find him, Tony?"

"Outside. Across the street. Watching your hotel. And waiting for you, or so he says," was Langley's curt reply. "Do you know the boy? He looks devilish familiar to me."

The lad flung himself into a chair, his hat pulled low over his face. Sulkily he said, "I told you he doesn't."

Coolly, Carswell addressed the boy. "You are supposed to be a cousin I don't know. How convenient for you."

"It ain't convenient," the boy retorted. "Leastways, I've never found it convenient to've been born the wrong side of the blanket."

"I see," Carswell said. He stood quite still for some moments before he abruptly turned to Langley and clapped his friend on the shoulder and added, "Thank you for bringing the boy up here, Tony. I rather think he *is* my cousin. By an uncle, I suppose, and I think I even know which one. But as this is apt to get rather, er, delicate, I shall have to send you on your way."

Amused, Langley replied, "My dear Carswell, I understand perfectly. You should see some of the skeletons in my family closet! Tomorrow, then, and don't forget."

"I shan't," Carswell agreed amiably, and held the door open for his friend to leave. When Langley was gone he turned back to the lad and addressed him in tones that stung like a whip. "Well, Miss Farnham? Are you going to tell me what this charade is all about? Or am I simply to assume you have lost all your wits and belong in Bedlam?"

"H—how did you know it was me?" she

demanded anxiously. "I thought I played the part
of a boy rather well. Your friend Major Langley
didn't guess anything was amiss."

Carswell snorted in exasperation. "He doesn't
know you as well as I do and if I didn't you might
even have fooled me. Where did you learn to walk
and talk like that? And why take such a risk? You
heard Langley—he found you devilish familiar.
Fortunately, it never occurred to him to match
your face to that of a certain gently bred young
lady he has met."

"An actress has to be prepared to play all sorts
of roles," Mary retorted loftily.

"Actress, be damned! What the devil are you
doing here dressed as a boy?" Carswell demanded.

"Would you rather I had come to call upon you
dressed as myself? A proper young lady?" Mary
countered innocently.

"I would rather you had not come to call at all,"
Carswell said witheringly. "I repeat: What are you
doing here?"

Mary rose to her feet, her eyes glittering with
anger. "I came to find out why you have all but
abandoned me."

In spite of himself, Carswell laughed. "I should
scarcely call it abandoning you," he protested, "to
have placed you in the care of a loving aunt and
uncle."

"You know very well what I mean," Mary said
evenly.

Carswell leaned against the mantle of the fireplace, his cane propped against the wall. "I
suppose you have convinced yourself you know
the answer already?" he asked calmly.

"Certainly," she replied, beginning to pace the
room. "You have somehow placed yourself in

disgrace with my uncle. By drinking and holding with bad company and being unwilling to pledge yourself not to do so again, I collect. But I wanted to discover if it was more than that. If you have taken me in dislike, perhaps."

Carswell meant to be cruel. He could not believe that either of them would be better served by the truth. But Mary Farnham had stopped pacing not more than a foot away from him, and now she looked at him with eyes that held his firmly and he found he could not do it. Instead, before he even knew what he was about, Carswell had folded her against his chest, his chin resting on the top of her head as he said in exasperation, "Why can't you be a conventional young lady and wait at home, as you ought, for me to call on you?"

A watery chuckle greeted this question and when he held her away from him to see her face, Carswell found the most delightful smile and dancing eyes staring up at him. "But you haven't come to call even once in the past two weeks," Mary protested. "Besides, you know I'm not a conventional young lady."

"I do know it. You're a damned little fool instead!" Carswell told her roundly. "You take risks you have no right to take."

"What risks?" Mary countered.

Carswell ran a hand through his hair. "Don't you understand? If some half-foxed gentleman were to realize your sex, you would find yourself in a great deal of trouble."

"I collect you mean I should find my reputation in shreds? As though I cared a fig for that!" Mary said scornfully.

"No, I am not talking about your reputation," Carswell retorted grimly. Then with a sigh of exasperation he shook her and said, "That half-foxed gentleman would very likely treat you something like this!"

Captain Carswell pulled Miss Farnham to him, tossed her hat on a chair, and ruthlessly kissed her. It seemed to Mary that his lips meant to punish her as his hands gripped her arms unrelentingly. When she tried to protest, he let one hand slide around her waist, pulling her even tighter to him, and the other roam familiarly over her body. And when he became frustrated by the bindings over her breasts the captain's hands abandoned them to stroke instead in her womanhood, unprotected now by skirts and petticoats.

Only when Carswell felt the tears begin to course down Mary's cheeks did he let her go. "That, Miss Farnham, is a taste of what you might have to endure if you were caught out in your masquerade," he said grimly.

Mortified, Mary replied, her voice quavering as she tried to lay claim to a certain bravado, "And is that, then, the much vaunted passion between the sexes?"

Even with the knowledge that to answer was madness, Carswell could not help himself. "No," he said as he reached for her once more, "this is."

Carswell's lips were gentle this time as they tasted the ripeness of Miss Farnham's mouth and his hands held her tenderly. Mary's own hands crept up the captain's back until they wound around his neck of their own accord and she leaned towards him, losing herself in his embrace. After what seemed to Mary far too short a time, Carswell resolutely pushed her away from him. His breath was a trifle ragged as he said, "You must go home now. I'll take you. And I want you to promise you shan't try this again."

"Only if you will promise to come and see me," Mary replied boldly.

"I shall when I can," he answered grimly.

"But—"

"But nothing," Carswell retorted. "If you won't promise, then I shall have to advise Mr. Foster to send you home again to Essex and I shall disappear so that you can't find me at all."

Mary stared at him, reading the determination in Carswell's eyes. "Very well," she said at last. "For the moment I promise I shall not call upon you again."

"Or go about in this disguise?" Carswell persisted.

"Or go about in this disguise," Mary agreed wearily. "But I do wish you would tell me what is afoot."

"All in good time," Carswell replied, retrieving her hat and placing it firmly upon her head. "Now come along and I'll take you home. I have some acquaintances I *must* meet a little later."

Meekly, Mary followed him.

They came out of the door of the Horn and Hare without talking, for both feared that Miss Farnham's voice would give her away. And indeed, Mary was grateful for the time to simply think about what had just occurred. Perhaps Captain Carswell was similarly preoccupied for he was as surprised as she was when the two men stepped out of the shadows.

"Good evening, Captain Carswell," the first addressed him.

"Who is your young friend?" the other asked.

They stopped and Carswell leaned heavily upon his cane. With an apparently lazy manner he replied, "Good evening, Dugard, Perrin. You are early. This lad? This is my young cousin. Though we don't generally recognize him as such. A living family skeleton, one might say."

The gaze of the two exiled Frenchmen swept without interest over Mary. "We thought you might like to join us for a drink, now, Captain Carswell," Dugard said off-handedly.

"I should be delighted," Carswell replied. "As soon as I have seen my cousin home."

"But no, he must come with us," Perrin protested goodnaturedly. "We shall introduce him— gently, of course, oh so gently—to the pleasures of wine and later perhaps women, eh, Dugard?"

"But certainly," Dugard agreed readily. "I should never forgive myself if we allowed the boy to go away to his bed alone so early in the evening."

"Come we shall have him home within the hour, if that is what you wish," Perrin coaxed, peering closely at Mary. Hastily Carswell stepped in front of her and said, "As you wish, though you've no one but yourselves to blame if the boy becomes a dead bore. Where are we off to? The Fox and Crown?"

"Why no," Dugard said with apparent surprise. "We managed to lay hands on a few bottles of exceptional wine as well as brandy and thought you might care to sample some. And, after all, our lodgings are so much, er, quieter than the Fox and Crown, as well as a trifle pleasanter."

Carswell quirked an eyebrow but all he said aloud was, "Very well, lead the way. Coming, Jeremy?"

As Mary correctly took this to be herself, she

nodded her head and followed meekly as the other three started off down the road, walking slowly in deference to the captain's injured leg.

A short time later they turned in at the door of one of the seedier lodging houses in Brighton. Perrin turned to the English pair and said, "You must not be thinking this is the best we can afford. But as we have no idea how long our exile from France will be, we think it best to conserve our funds."

"Besides," Dugard added silkily, "no one is likely to bother us here or object to the sound of voices late into the morning hours. Everyone in this building is remarkably discreet, you will find."

None of this quelled in any way Captain Carswell's sense of unease. Particularly not the speculative gazes his companions turned on young "Jeremy" from time to time. But there was nothing to be done except to follow Dugard and Perrin up the narrow staircase to the top floor where they had their apartment. The chaotic state of these rooms, in marked contrast to the neatness of Perrin's and Dugard's persons, led Carswell to narrow his eyes in thought. "Jeremy" merely wrinkled his nose, a gesture not lost on their hosts.

"Why the poor boy is far too fastidious, Dugard," Perrin told his friend. "Really, captain, you must teach him better manners."

Carswell shrugged and raised an eyebrow. "That young puppy?" he asked in disbelief. "I have no responsibility toward him. As for his manners, you are quite right in saying they are atrocious. But what can one expect of family by-blows?"

Once more the two Frenchmen stared speculatively at Jeremy, causing the lad to fling himself sulkily in a chair. "Roast me all you wish," he said roughly, "but I tell you, your family does have a responsibility toward me!"

Carswell laughed harshly. "I shall much enjoy watching you try to take that line with my father! You'll find yourself out the door, on your ear, in five minutes' time. *If* he is feeling kindly."

"We shall see," was all the boy replied.

As he watched the quarreling with a shrewd eye, Dugard brought out a bottle of brandy and poured each of his guests a glass. Miss Farnham dared not refuse and in character as Jeremy sipped carelessly at her brandy. With a wry quirk of the lips she silently acknowledged just how thoroughly she must be ruining herself in Captain Carswell's eyes. Certainly he watched her consume the brandy with a most disapproving expression upon his face. He was not to know that this was not Mary's first encounter with such potables. Mary's stepbrother had delighted in forcing her to taste brandy and port and even blue ruin over the last few months before she ran away. It had been useless to try to complain to her mother. As for her stepfather, he had only observed that he did not believe in raising girls as though they were hothouse blooms and what were a few high spirits in a lad her stepbrother's age? Now Mary had reason to be grateful that he had forced her to taste the stuff because otherwise she would most certainly have been unable to conceal her ignorance of their taste or effect.

As the last of these thoughts crossed Mary's mind, she began to feel a trifle unwell. She slumped forward with a half-spoken apology and Carswell, with an oath, took a step toward her before he, too, slumped to the floor. Dugard and Perrin looked at one another with satisfied smiles before Dugard broke out another bottle, this time claret, and the pair of them sat down to serious drinking while they waited for a hired man to arrive with a coach some hours later.

12

MARY Farnham came awake with a groan. The headache she had pretended the night before was now become a grim reality. She tried to reach for her head and then came abruptly full awake as she realized her hands were bound behind her. Taking a deep breath she slowly looked around trying to orient herself and discover where she was as well as whether Captain Carswell was with her. She seemed to be in a jolting carriage, laid out on the floor, and someone, perhaps Carswell, lay beside her. By the sound of the slow, steady breathing she decided he must be alive but not awake. And although there were curtains over the windows of the carriage, it seemed to Miss Farnham that she saw the first streaks of daylight peeking through.

So it was already almost morning, she thought grimly. And what would Uncle Hubert and Aunt Gwendolyn think when they discovered she was gone? Would they try to pay a call upon Captain Carswell at his hotel? If so, what would they think when they discovered he was gone as well?

For a moment Miss Farnham closed her eyes.

The knowledge that she would not have been in this situation had she not insisted upon paying a highly irregular call upon Captain Carswell did nothing to ease her fear or her guilt. There would be no avoiding scandal now. Not unless she managed to return to Brighton at once, which seemed unlikely even if she did manage to get free and find transportation, for she had to assume they had been traveling most of the night.

A groan beside Mary recalled her attention to the immediate situation and she whispered softly, "Captain Carswell? Is that you? Are you awake?"

For a long moment there was no sound and then a blistering curse answered her. When he had done with that, Captain Carswell spoke cautiously. "Jeremy? Is that you?"

Silently, Mary gave a prayer of thanks that the captain appeared to have his wits about him. "Yes, it's me," she answered, still whispering. "My hands are tied, what about you?"

"Hands and feet," he replied heavily. "And I can't see a thing. Where are we?"

Concern gave Mary the resolution to force herself to turn over in spite of the crampedness of their situation. She let out a sigh of relief when she saw that the captain wore a blindfold. "We're in a carriage, headed I'm not sure where. I suppose the brandy was drugged," she added a trifle bitterly. Taking a deep breath she went on, "They've tied us both up and put a blindfold on you. I suppose they consider you more dangerous than me. And, oh yes, it appears to be almost morning."

Carswell gave another curse. "Perrin and Dugard? Are they with us as well?"

"Not in the carriage,' Mary said uncertainly,

looking around once more. "But I suppose they might be riding alongside. I really don't know much; I've only just come awake myself so I've no idea how long we've been traveling or—or anything."

Carswell caught the note of apology in her voice and said roughly, "You've done well . . . Jeremy. If there is blame to be apportioned, it goes to me. I ought to have found some way to get you out of this before they managed to drug us."

"Let's just try to get out of this now," Mary replied firmly, tugging at her bonds.

For a moment Carswell didn't reply, then with an oath he told her, "They've tied me too securely. What about you?"

Mary, whose head was now throbbing worse than ever, could only say, "I can't undo mine either. But what good would it do if we could? We'd still be in a moving carriage."

"Yes, but with some chance of surprising our captors when the coach stopped," Carswell told her patiently. He hesitated, then added, "We cannot know if they have discovered your sex yet, but if not, let us try to postpone that discovery as long as possible. We are fortunate you did not rely upon a wig or your hat to hide your hair, for that would certainly have given you away by now. Daylight still might, though if we are fortunate they will be in a hurry to get us inside somewhere and not be looking too closely at your appearance. And you are, after all it seems, a talented actress. Still, even when we are alone I mean to call you Jeremy."

Mary nodded, forgetting he could not see her. Then, aloud she asked, trying to keep her voice steady, "What do you think they mean to do with us?"

"That depends upon what they know," Carswell replied cryptically. "But we can be certain they mean us to stay alive or we would never have woken from effects of the brandy. What I don't understand is why they have taken us so far away from Brighton."

Even as they spoke the carriage drew to a halt. Both passengers lay very still as the door was opened and two unfamiliar voices spoke.

"I 'ope they're awake," the first one said. "I've no mind to be draggin' them out the way we dragged them in."

"I'd ruther drag them than 'ave a fight on our 'ands," the second one replied tartly.

"Coo, after what the guvnor give them they'll not be in a state to fight," the first one retorted. Then, to Carswell and Mary he said, "All right, all right, on your feet, then. Come on, wake up now."

Slowly, groaning, Mary and the captain managed to sit, no easy feat with bound hands and the cramped quarters of the carriage floor. The two men helped first Mary, then the captain out of the carriage. With a sickening feeling, Mary saw him stumble without his cane. She looked about her and noted that they seemed to have been driven round to the back of some country building. Mary had no time to see any more before their captors pushed the pair toward an open door. "Inside and be quick about it!" the second one hissed. "No looking around, just go!"

Miss Farnham and Captain Carswell did as they were told, stumbling across the threshold into the welcome dimness of the interior. "Why 'asn't that one got a blindfold?" one of their captors asked.

"Aw, 'e don't matter. Just a boy, can't you see?" the other one replied. Then, to Mary and Carswell he said, "Behind you is a door down to the cellar.

That's where you'll be staying. Easy now, wouldn't
want you to have a nasty fall!"

That seemed such a funny notion to the two men
that it was some time before they could stop
laughing and each take one of the captives to guide
down the narrow steps to the room at the bottom,
where there was another door. Once inside the
cellar room Mary swiftly looked around. There
was the narrowest of slits allowing in light near
the roof of the room, and the door through which
they had entered. No other openings were visible.
The room itself was furnished with a crude table,
several chairs, three mattresses that looked as
though they were stuffed with straw, a sort of
screen at the back of the room, and chamber pots
by the beds.

"Not what you're accustomed to, I'll be bound,
but then you won't have been expecting luxury,"
the first captor said, setting himself and his
companion to laughing once more.

"I should be better able to judge if you would
remove my blindfold," Carswell said with cool
irony. "Unless you've some objection to my seeing
your faces."

"It's not that," the captor replied, "it's that we
thought you'd be less likely to try anything,
troublewise, if your eyes was covered. We'll have
that off in a flash."

When Carswell's eyes were free he, too, looked
about the room and then nodded with an air of
grim satisfaction. "It'll do," he said quietly.

"There, now, didn't I say he was a gen'lemun?"
the first captor said to the second.

"Gentleman enough for you to untie my
wrists?" Carswell asked mildly.

"Not likely," the second captor said hastily.
"The guv'nors said we wasn't to trust you a bit."

"What about the boy, then?" Carswell persisted. "He's hardly a threat."

"Oh, aye, and 'ow long would it take for 'im to untie you?" the first captor asked sarcastically. "You must take us for a green pair of flats! No, you'll both stay neatly tied until the guv'nors 'ave seen you and said different."

With those words the two men turned and left, carefully locking the heavy door behind them. Carswell looked at Mary and said, with heavy irony, "Care to have a seat, Jeremy?"

She shrugged, playing for an audience she suspected might still be behind the door. "Why not? Well, captain, what do you expect to happen next?"

Carswell's eyes strayed briefly to the door, betraying the fact that he too had heard no footsteps going up the stairs. "I haven't the faintest notion," he said coolly, also easing himself into a chair. "Nor do I greatly care. Certain, er, pressing debts in Brighton make it convenient for me to be out of town just now. And I fancy no one will much care where you are. This is just one of Perrin and Dugard's jokes, no doubt, and once they've come and had a laugh at us, they'll let us go. Certainly they don't mean to seriously mistreat us. After all, however crude these quarters are, they are certainly adequate."

"Adequate!" Mary gasped in outrage.

"Why yes," Carswell replied blandly. "Far better than most I had when I was in the Peninsula. So long as they don't mean to starve us I shan't complain."

Still in character as the sulky youth, Mary slouched in her chair and said, "Well, I shall! I want some food and I want it now!"

The two prisoners paused to listen but there

was no response from beyond the door. But when the silence had stretched on for ten minutes the two guards apparently gave up their post for Mary and Captain Carswell were able to hear two pairs of feet trying to ascend the steps quietly.

When they were gone Mary looked at Carswell and said, "Are you all right without your cane?"

"I'll manage," he replied curtly.

She nodded, then asked hesitantly, "Do you believe what you said just now?"

Carswell looked at Mary. Had she made the least effort to evade his eyes he would cheerfully have lied to her. But she did not. So after a long moment he said, "No. That is to say, I believe they will not harm us. At least for now. But this is not a joke. Even if the accommodations are somewhat better than I expected."

Soberly Mary nodded. "And I am an added complication. For them and for you."

Carswell nodded. "But because they believe you are in some sort related to me, they will not harm you so long as they do not harm me."

"And for how long will that be?" Mary asked quietly.

"I don't know," Carswell answered honestly. "I have some notion, though no certainty, what they want. And it may be that I can contrive to hold them off for a time and even get us out of here. But I make no promises to that effect."

"I understand," Mary replied calmly. "It is after all my own fault I'm here. And my responsibility to help if I can. But how?"

"Simply continue to be my scapegrace, illegitimate cousin," Carswell said. "For both our sakes they must continue to believe that tale." He paused and smiled wryly. "How fortunate the light is so dim here and how fortunate that they never met your other self. Though I'll allow your mastery of the part is amazing. If I didn't know better, you might have fooled me. Briefly."

"I once thought I would make my living on the stage," Mary said soberly. "I wanted to be an expert at every conceivable part."

"You never did tell me really why you ran away from home," Carswell said quietly. "You told me you weren't happy there, but that is scarcely a sufficient answer. I might have thought it was when I thought you had run off to join the theater as a lark. But now I can see matters went far deeper than that. You must have given the matter much thought and spent a good many months preparing to run away. Why?"

Mary hesitated. For all her desire to be an actress and her talent for playing a part, it was not in her nature to lie, particularly not to the man who sat across from her. Moreover, at the moment propriety and her reputation seemed not very important given that there seemed a good chance she might soon die. In the end Mary opted for the truth. "I have told you before that my stepfather disliked me. As for my mother, she was indifferent. To be fair, neither liked their other children much better; they were far too involved in their own affairs to be concerned about ours. Indeed, until this past year or so they spent every spring in London. You may even have met them there. My stepfather's name is Gerald Kensley."

Mary paused long enough to see Carswell's nod of agreement, then she went on, "As a result, my stepbrothers and half brothers and I were much thrown together. At first we were friends. They did not disdain to play with me and include me in their games, even climbing ladders and pretending to storm forts.

"But things changed after a while. The younger ones were still all right, it was the eldest who was the problem. He was no more than a year younger than I and far stronger. It was his notion to taunt me. To tie my hands and force brandy and gin down my throat. Or to strand me in a distant field afterward, one to which he had taken me blind-folded so that I didn't know where I was. Then he would purposely start off in the wrong direction to mislead me.

"Once he put a dead cat in my bed. Another time I found he had poisoned my favorite among the dogs. I tried to tell my mother but she did not wish to hear it. My stepfather only laughed and said his son was merely a lively young boy and that such tricks would help to keep me from becoming a milk-and-water chit, something he said he could not abide."

Mary shuddered and then went on, "Over the last few months I was home the tricks began to grow more frightening. My stepbrother even began to talk of how we were not truly related. That there was no real bar to a marriage between us. I knew that was nonsense, but he began to talk of teaching me to be his wife and I knew I must run away.

"You once called me hopelessly naive because I did not know the dangers of the theater. You were right. But you are naive if you believe they are worse than the ones I faced in my own home."

Carswell stared for a long moment at Mary without answering. Already pale, she went lighter still until she thought she might faint. There was no doubt, she thought, that the look in his eyes held contempt and horror for her. However little the events that had occurred might have been her fault, nevertheless they had still tainted her beyond redemption for anyone who was a member of the *ton*. Mary Farnham had gambled that Captain Carswell might be sufficiently different to listen without condemning her. His silence, however, told her she had been mistaken. Too late she remembered the vicar she had once ventured to tell, who had told her to go home and never speak of such things again lest she be either shunned or clapped into Bedlam as a lunatic for telling such improbable tales. Trembling slightly she said with dignity, "So you see, you needn't have worried what damage might have been done me by a career in the theater since I should scarcely have been considered marriageable in any event."

Very quietly Carswell replied, "Do you know, I think it is a great pity dueling has gone out of style. But then, perhaps I just ought to take a horse whip to your stepfather and your step-brother. Do you think you would care to watch?"

13

"**WHAT** I cannot understand," Captain Carswell said a few moments later with a frown, "is why you should ever have considered what they did to have been your fault."

In spite of everything, Mary Farnham found she could not meet his eyes. "I did not say that I considered it my fault," she corrected him gently. "I merely said that it set me apart, made me unmarriageable. You cannot deny that few men would wish to marry me if they knew my history. Particularly if they knew that marriage to me would mean that my stepbrother would publicly try to embarrass us. He once told me," she said in the same steady tone, "that if I ever married anyone else he would tell the *ton* that he and I had been lovers."

"He would not have done that," Carswell said incredulously. "That would have ruined him as well. And as your stepfather's heir, he would have wished to marry and have children of his own. Something that would not have been possible if he did as you say. No, I think that must have been an idle threat and you were foolish enough to believe it."

Now Mary met the captain's eyes squarely as she said, still in an even tone, "I have known for some time that madness ran in my stepbrother's blood and my stepfather's. A madness they were careful always to conceal, save when alone among the family. My stepbrother would not have cared that he ruined his chances for marriage. If need be, my stepfather would have bought him a wife as he bought my mother for himself."

At Carswell's looks of surprise Mary laughed a trifle bitterly. "Oh yes, my mother married him because of his money. She did not like being poor and my father tied up the inheritance for me with only an income for her during her lifetime. Some might have considered it a very generous income, but my mother talked as though he had left her all but destitute. And so when my stepfather, who had been named a trustee of the estate, courted her and offered to marry her and make her wealthy again, my mother accepted. She did not care how eccentric he might be so long as she always had the money she needed for new dresses and jewels and every treat her heart was ever set on."

"You are very harsh on your mother," Carswell observed quietly.

Mary stared at him. "She should have protected me. But she did not because she was never willing to risk my stepfather's anger or the possibility that he would tie shut the purse strings. I do believe I hate her for that."

"Perhaps your mother felt she had no choice," Carswell countered.

Mary tilted her chin up. "Some people might have said that I had no choice either. But I did have a choice and I made it. I am not lying to you when I say that I would rather have starved trying

to be an actress than gone back home again." She
hesitated, then added softly, "I cannot, I will not
believe that there are ever no choices. They may
not always accord with what one wishes or what
society approves of, but I have found that these
things are luxuries one cannot always afford."

"But your choice might have landed you in a
situation far worse than your present one,"
Carswell observed.

"And is that a reason not to have made it?" Mary
flung back at him in anger. "Had my first choice
been a mistake I would have made another choice.
And another and another until a solution was
found. But I would never have simply accepted a
situation that was so wrong."

"You might have gone to your Aunt Gwendolyn
at once instead of trying to run first to the
theater," Carswell pointed out meekly.

Mary regarded the captain with no little bitterness. "How easily you say that. And I cannot deny
that you are right. But I had not seen her in ten
years and I was afraid she was too much like my
mother." Now Mary leaned forward as she went
on earnestly, "I did the best I could. Certainly
there might have been more sensible choices to
make, but who was there to advise me? The local
vicar? He counseled me to be a good daughter. My
mother wanted no knowledge of my trouble. Who
could I have asked? I am not stupid. I knew there
were risks in what I was doing. But I did the best I
could!"

Carswell nodded. Soberly he said, "I do know it
and I admire your courage."

"Now your turn," Mary said grimly. "Tell me
why you didn't come to call for two weeks—and I
don't mean because my aunt and uncle asked you

not to. You said at Prinny's party that I was not to confuse illusion with reality and I want to know what you meant."

Carswell groaned. "I must have had too much to drink," he said. "All right, I'll tell you. I was afraid something like this might happen and I didn't want you mixed up in it."

"You thought something like this might happen?" Mary repeated slowly in disbelief.

Mary had no time to ask any more questions, however, because scarcely had she finished speaking when they heard the sound of a carriage pulling into the yard. The slits near the ceiling allowed in noise and a little light but were not large enough to allow either Mary or Carswell to see who might have arrived. They had little doubt, however, that it was Perrin or Dugard or both. "Let me do the talking," Carswell warned Mary quickly. "They must not guess who you are."

She nodded, then tried to slouch further down in her chair as she waited.

It was more than a few minutes later when the door to the cellar prison opened to admit Perrin and Dugard. "Jeremy" lounged sulkily in his chair while Captain Carswell sat quite coolly in his.

Perrin came forward with a bow and said, "A thousand apologies, my friends! I am desolate to see you so uncomfortable."

Jeremy snorted and Carswell merely raised an eyebrow.

"But you do not believe me?" Perrin asked with mock surprise. "I shall give you proof. As soon as Dugard and I leave, your, er, guardians have orders to untie your hands."

"How generous," Carswell murmured sarcastically.

"But we are," Dugard protested. "The beds you will find quite comfortable, I am sure. You have a table and chairs and even a screen for privacy should either of you desire such. What more could you wish?"

"Let us go," Jeremy muttered softly.

Dugard regarded the "boy." "Ah, once more we are desolate because we cannot grant your request. It is a great pity you chose last night to call upon your kinsman."

"Too right!" the lad muttered.

"But you were expecting someone to accompany me," Carswell pointed out, "judging by the fact that there is more than one bed and by the screen."

Dugard coughed and looked away. Perrin, however, was not in the least disconcerted. He took a chair and faced Carswell as he said, "You are extremely perceptive, are you not? Ah, well, one would have had to tell you soon enough anyway. Yes, you were expected to have company here, but not right away. We shall perhaps have to acquire an additional bed."

He paused and waited, and after a moment Carswell murmured, "My apologies for disrupting your plans. Do you mean to tell me what they are?"

Perrin stared at his immaculately groomed nails and then replied, "You have retired, have you not, from the military and are somewhat at loose ends?"

"Yes, but it shouldn't have been that way," Carswell answered, his voice beginning to rise in anger. "I could still have worked but those fools in the War Office said they had no use for cripples like me. Go home, they said! Even my old friends seem to think I'm of no use anymore. The lot of them be damned!"

Perrin spread his hands. "But of a certainty they are fools! You are outraged, my friend, and you have every right to be. All I ask, then, is something in accord with your own feelings. Let us play a trick on some of these old friends who have turned their backs on you."

"What sort of trick?" Carswell asked suspiciously.

Dugard clicked his tongue in disapproval. "You do not trust us," he said sadly. "But we mean *you* no harm."

"Do as we ask and not only will we happily set you free but will make you a richer man by perhaps five hundred pounds as well," Perrin concluded with an ingratiating smile.

Carswell seemed to hesitate. At last he said uneasily, "What is it you wish me to do? And where does my cousin Jeremy come into this?"

Dugard spread his hands helplessly. "He was with you and we could not leave him behind to raise an alarm or to tell anyone where you had gone."

"But you know," Perrin said thoughtfully, "we may have a use for the boy, after all."

To her credit, Mary did not betray by the slightest movement her alarm at these words. Nor did Carswell. After a moment Perrin went on. "It occurs to me that we might send your cousin with a message to your friends. Then they will know it came from you."

Carswell laughed harshly. "They are more likely to throw the boy out on his ear. Langley is the only one who has met Jeremy and *he* distrusts the boy altogether."

Perrin shrugged. "As you will," he said. "Then I suppose you must write a letter to your friends asking them to come here."

"And if you refuse," Dugard said with exaggerated sadness, "we shall be forced to kill both of you and that would be a thousand pities."

"Refuse!" The word seemed to explode from Carswell's lips. "Refuse to give those fellows their comeuppance? After their *kind* condescension? Scarcely!" Abruptly he stopped, frowned, then asked more quietly, "But what do you want them here for? It's not . . . not anything treasonous, is it?"

It was Dugard's turn to snort. "You are shot in the leg by your own men," he said, holding Carswell's eyes with his own, "discarded like a useless old boot by others, declared an outcast by your family, your heroism ignored by the entire country, and you worry about treason? No, my friend, it is not to be believed!"

"But is it treasonous?" Carswell persisted.

Dugard would have answered but Perrin held up a hand to forestall him. Quietly he said, "My friend, there are many words that mean many things to many people. I will not lie to you. What I ask you to do, some would call treason. I do not. I am neither on England's side nor on France's side. I am on the side of sanity. Too many men have died already and others like yourself left wounded in a world that has no place for such. Have you seen how many crippled beggars—old soldiers— wander the streets of London, wondering if they will even find bread for the day?

"I tell you there must be an end to this war. And to all wars. And I believe that your friends may help me in this. The information they carry can end the war *if* it reaches the right hands. I can help it to do so. But you must help me if we are to put an end to this insane madness."

Slowly Carswell nodded. "There is no glory in men starving in rain-drenched huts or lying near death on muddy battlefields," he said. "And for what? A little bit of land that will only be fought over again a dozen times in the next hundred years? I'll help you all right, just tell me what to do." Carswell paused and looked at Jeremy with something akin to contempt. "You'll no doubt applaud my doing this even if you don't understand my reasons. You think anything is acceptable so long as it is to your own benefit. That's all you care about!"

Jeremy merely shrugged and Carswell turned away with a snort of disgust. To Perrin the captain added sharply, "I'll need paper, pen, and ink and you'll need to untie my hands so that I can write." He hesitated, then added quietly, "And could I have my cane. It is difficult for me to get around without it."

Perrin spread his hands. "I am desolate, but I cannot allow you your cane. As for the other things, but of course."

With a word Dugard went upstairs to fetch what was needed. As they waited Perrin said in a conversational tone, "You will forgive me, I know, if I take the precaution of keeping you a prisoner here until your friends, and their information, are safely in my hands." Carswell nodded and Perrin went on, "Your kinsman as well. Unless, of course, you would wish me to get rid of him for you?"

Carswell shook his head but without haste or alarm. "Leave the boy. He is becoming, in some sort I fear, my responsibility even if he was born the wrong side of the blanket. I do not despair of knocking some sense into him, given time, and if I succeed I've some plans for the boy."

Perrin looked from one to the other. With a shrug he said, "As you wish."

A moment later Dugard returned to the cellar prison with paper, pen, ink, a candle, and one of the jailors. Perrin immediately rose to his feet and bowed to Carswell. "I leave you to your task now for, let us say, half an hour. Then I must be off to Brighton. Social engagements, you know. You will please to ask your friends Langley and Wollcott to come to the village of Lullington. For what urgent reason I leave to your fertile imagination. And if you can persuade them to bring their papers, all the better. Though if not—" Perrin paused and shrugged. "If not, I still do not despair of persuading your friends to tell us where to find them. One of my, er, employees is an expert in such matters."

Carswell noted that Dugard could not entirely suppress a shudder at these words. The captain's face, however, betrayed nothing as he said mildly, "My bonds? I cannot write with my hands tied behind me."

"As soon as we are safely beyond the door," Perrin explained courteously. He coughed and added, "I fear I am becoming overly cautious these days, but of a certainty I know you will understand and forgive me."

Carswell inclined his head and waited. As Perrin had said, once the two Frenchmen were outside the room, the jailor cut Carswell's hands free. Immediately the captain flexed them, then began to rub his wrists as the jailor hastily left the cellar room as well.

Through all this Mary Farnham regarded Captain Carswell with the sulky expression habitual to Jeremy. Nor did she make the least effort to interrupt him as he wrote the letter commanded by Perrin and Dugard—a restraint for which Carswell was profoundly grateful. Most of the half hour was spent composing the letter in his head and it was some time before he even put pen to paper to begin.

> My Dear Tony,
>   I have found the most delightful village imaginable, called Lullington. All of your favorite delights, and Jack's, are to be found here and were I not such a selfish fellow, I would urge you to make haste to get here as soon as possible.
>   Yes, yes, I know you've work to do, but bring it along. I assure you, you will not regret the detour.
>   Yours,
>   Captain Randall Carswell

At last Carswell leaned back in his chair with a sigh of satisfaction. He held up the paper and read the note aloud to Jeremy, who scarcely seemed to hear a word of it. When he was done, Carswell asked carelessly, "Well, Jeremy? What do you think of it?"

A trifle petulantly the boy shrugged and said, "It's all one to me. I just want to get out of here."

"And so we shall, soon enough, I'll wager," Carswell said kindly. "My friends will arrive shortly and then Perrin and Dugard are certain to let us go." Jeremy gave a snort. "You don't believe me," Carswell went on, still in his kindly manner, "but so long as I am likely to be of future use to them they will not hurt us."

Scarcely had Carswell finished speaking when their jailor opened the cellar door and came forward to take the letter from Carswell. He untied Jeremy's wrists as well. At Jeremy's look of surprise the fellow shrugged and said, "Them's the orders, young sir. No 'ard feelings, I 'ope?"

For an answer Jeremy merely glared at the man, who laughed. "Regular little fighting fellow, ain't you?" he said. "I likes a boy with spirit."

Then he left with the candle, pen, ink, and letter, and Jeremy and Carswell were once more alone. Jeremy rubbed his wrists, carefully avoiding the captain's eyes, and so he did not see the amusement that briefly flared in them. When Carswell judged that his young companion's circulation had been adequately restored and he had also heard Perrin and Dugard's coach pull out of the yard, he leaned forward and said quietly, "I think we have some plans to make."

14

JACK Wollcott, Anthony Langley, and Viscount Halliwell were in the midst of an early game of cards after dinner when the letter arrived from Carswell, delivered by an unknown messenger boy. "What is it, Tony?" Wollcott asked after his friend had had time to peruse the missive.

Without haste Langley refolded the paper and handed it over to Wollcott. For Halliwell's benefit he explained with a laugh, "It seems that Carswell had found himself in a very diverting place. A village called Lullington. Wants Jack and me to join him there."

"Shall I come along?" Halliwell asked as he watched Wollcott finish reading the note.

"Why not," Langley said with a shrug. "How about you, Jack?"

"Wish I could. Carswell has a nose for such things," the captain replied. "Unfortunately I've a prior engagement for midnight. With a young, er, lady."

"Come with us. From the looks of Carswell's letter there are plenty of, er, young ladies where he is," Langley urged. "When has he ever let us down?"

Wollcott hesitated, then shrugged. "Why not. The lady in question will soon find other consolation, I've no doubt, and I'd begun to tire of her anyway. When do we leave?"

"Why not right now?" Halliwell urged.

Langley appeared to consider the matter. "Why not, indeed?" he agreed. "Let's each pack a small bag, and if you will get your phaeton, Freddy, we can be off within the hour. How does that sound?"

"Splendid. Absolutely splendid," Halliwell agreed.

"I can't wait to see what Randall has found for us this time," Wollcott added with a smile.

The three men rose, Langley paid the shot for the drinks they had had while playing cards, and they left the club. A pair of interested eyes watched their departure with great satisfaction and the fellow hurried off to inform his employer that the coves in question had quit the club and appeared to be planning to leave town. Perrin and Dugard did not wait any longer but made their own arrangements to return to Lullington as quickly as possible, this time by horseback instead of by carriage.

The Foster household was, some hours later, still in an uproar. Fortunately for Mary the staff was extremely discreet and no word of her disappearance had leaked to the *ton*. That did not mean, however, that Hubert and Gwendolyn Foster were any less distressed. In fact, Gwendolyn and her husband were discussing Mary's disappearance after returning from a dinner engagement they had felt it wiser not to break.

"Any word?" Gwendolyn asked her majordomo as soon as they were back in their own house.

He bowed. "I'm very sorry but there has been none, ma'am," he replied. "As you requested, the maid has made another check of Miss Farnham's wardrobe and she repeats that none of Miss Farnham's things are missing."

"But dash it all, she cannot have gone out in her nightdress," Hubert protested. "Unless she was abducted from her bed."

The majordomo coughed. "As to that, sir, I believe that not even her nightdress is missing."

"Stark naked?" Hubert said, his eyes rounding in shock. "Surely you cannot mean that you think she went out without a stitch on her back?"

"No, sir. Right now the maid is engaged in questioning the servants to discover if Miss Farnham borrowed or attempted to borrow clothing from any of them."

As he spoke, the maid appeared. Sketching a quick curtsy she said to Gwendolyn, "I think ma'am, I may have the answer. Miss Farnham, when she first come here, left a parcel with the youngest footman. Yesterday she asked him for it back and he give it to her."

"And said nothing to anyone?" Hubert asked with a frown.

The maid curtsied again and said hastily, "Well, sir, he didn't think anything of it. Then. Seemed just a favor to her. He had no idea what might be in the parcel 'cept now he thinks it may have been clothes on account of how none of Miss Farnham's is missing and the parcel was pretty soft and all."

"Yes, I see. Thank you, Sara," Hubert said heavily. The maid turned to go but, as an afterthought he stopped her and asked, "Miss Farnham didn't happen to tell the boy where she was going or what she planned to do, did she?"

The maid shook her head. "No, sir. But Kevin says she did seem very determined about something. And he said to say he's very sorry for the trouble and that he didn't tell you beforehand."

Hubert waved a careless hand. "Oh, it's not his fault. Obviously, my minx of a niece simply used him and he had no reason to suspect anything was afoot. Certainly her aunt and I did not. I just wish we knew where she could be."

That was a question Gwendolyn echoed a few minutes later when they were alone in the drawing room. "Are you certain she didn't go to see Captain Carswell?" Gwendolyn asked, a glass of wine in her hand.

"Positive," Hubert replied. "I spoke with the clerk at his hotel. No young ladies, no ladies at all, called upon Captain Carswell last night or this morning. And he himself left with a young boy, some sort of relative, the clerk thought, last night and has not been back since, although he has not paid his shot and his things are still there. Family business, I shouldn't wonder. I did think Mary might have gone after him except that no young lady was seen or heard asking for him or where he could be. Not that anyone knew."

"Perhaps Mary already knew," Gwendolyn suggested quietly.

"Perhaps, though I cannot think how. Carswell obeyed our request, so far as I can be sure, not to have any contact with her," Hubert said. "In any event, even if she knew where he was, we do not, so that scarcely helps us."

"We could write to Lord Atley and ask if Captain Carswell has any family near Brighton," Gwendolyn suggested.

"Yes, and in the morning I shall," Hubert agreed. "In the meanwhile, what the devil shall we do? Suppose she turns up on the stage of the Brighton theater and someone recognizes her? At this point I wouldn't put anything past the girl."

Gwendolyn was practical. "We must hope Mary does not," she said. "Somehow, I do not think it likely, thought she may have sought out a country company somewhere else. In any event, until we do discover her whereabouts I suppose we shall just have to do our best to keep anyone from realizing what has occurred. Under ordinary circumstances I should have tried to keep it from the servants, but in this case, it was impossible. If only I hadn't told Sara to come upstairs with me this morning to check on Mary!"

"Hmm," Hubert said rubbing his chin. "Yes, well, can't be helped. Don't fret, m'dear. If Mary's gone any length of time at all we would have needed their cooperation anyway. You could hardly have taken the line that she'd left to go and stay with someone else when every stitch of clothing she owns is still here as well as her favorite brushes and combs and things. By the by, what did you tell Lady Dunsmore?"

"I told her that Mary had a touch of fever and was laid down in her bed," Gwendolyn said with some satisfaction. "So long as none of the servants talk, and I don't think they shall, we have bought ourselves a few days with that tale." She stopped, sighed, then added, "I suppose we are fortunate in one thing. No one seems to have seen her out by herself last night or the gossip would already have begun and Lady Dunsmore, if anyone, would have heard and rushed to repeat it to me. Instead, she was all eagerness to discover if I meant to go on a diet as she said I appeared to have gained some weight."

Gwendolyn ended with a laugh, one that Hubert heartily shared. Sitting down beside his wife he gently patted her stomach. "And how is the little one today?" he asked with fatherly pride.

"Quiet," Gwendolyn confided with a smile. "For which I am very grateful. Sometimes I think the child means to kick its way out well before its time!"

"There's nothing wrong with you or the child, is there?" Hubert asked anxiously. "Because it's quiet, I mean."

Gwendolyn stroked her husband's cheek. "Not in the least," she assured him. "I expect that even this baby needs to sleep sometime. Speaking of sleep, shall we go up to bed now? You've said yourself that there is nothing more we can do until morning."

Hubert caught his wife's hand to his lips and, looking into her eyes, a smile playing about his mouth, he said, "Well, let us go up to bed, at any rate."

Meanwhile, the Marquess of Alnwick arrived in Brighton.

15

THE three friends, Langley, Wollcott, and Halliwell, arrived at the small inn in Lullington shortly before midnight. Although a number of local people were there, Captain Randall Carswell was nowhere to be seen. Looking about him Halliwell said, with no little astonishment, "Whatever was Carswell thinking of to recommend this place so highly? And for that matter, where the deuce is he?"

Wollcott was more amused. "No doubt he found some agreeable company and that blinded him to all other considerations," he said easily. "In any event, so long as we are here, why not have something to drink? I confess that my throat is rather parched and perhaps the innkeeper has seen Randall."

"Excellent notion," Langley agreed. "Let's ask him."

When applied to, however, the innkeeper denied all knowledge of an ex-military gentleman with an injured leg.

"Well, but this is Lullington, isn't it?" Wollcott demanded.

" 'Course it is," the innkeeper said. "But I tell you I've seen no one of that description. Has anyone here?"

"I 'ave," said a solidly built fellow. "Over t'other side of the fields. Staying wi' an acquaintance, 'e said, 'oo'd rented the grand cottage, the one that use t'be an inn."

"Oh, aye, I mind now," the innkeeper said slowly. "Keep to themselves, they do. Never even dropping in of an evening to sample my brew, which is the best hereabouts."

He paused and looked at the three gentlemen. Langley, taking the hint at once, ordered for himself and his friends. When they were served, the major carried his glass over to the table where the solid fellow was sitting and said easily, "I don't suppose you'd care to show us the way, a little later, after we've finished our drinks?"

The fellow shrugged. "I don't see as why not. Particular if 'ee was to wet my throat first. Shouldn't like to try to find my way with thirstiness on m'mind."

With an amused laugh Langley ordered a pint of the innkeeper's home brew for the solid fellow as well. "Might I know your name?" he asked.

Since the fellow was busy gulping from his mug, the innkeeper answered for him. "His name is Mike. And though there's not many hereabouts have a good word for him I reckon he'll help you find your way, right enough. So long as you hold him to the one pint."

Mike gave the innkeeper a reproachful look but ten minutes later he was clumsily trying to climb into the saddle of a rather broken-down nag. After his third unsuccessful attempt Wollcott snorted with impatience. "Oh, the devil with it. Let's take him up with us and he can direct us on our way."

"We'll be a trifle crowded," Halliwell observed.

"What of it? He can ride in the groom's spot," Langley replied. "Besides, we can survive anything for a short time. I presume, Mike, this grand cottage *is* nearby."

"Oh, yes, sir, and thank 'ee, sir," Mike said, making haste to take Wollcott up upon the offer.

True to his word, he had them there in twenty minutes, using, as Langley later said, "the damndest collection of back roads and lanes" he had ever seen. At any rate they arrived and Mike directed them to drive round back of the now-dark house.

"P'rhaps it's too late to call and we ought to go back to the inn," Halliwell suggested.

"No, no, I'll warrant they'll be happy to see any friends of the military gen'lemun," Mike assured them solemnly. "A great favorite 'e is wi' 'em."

So Langley drove around back as directed into a small courtyard behind the cottage. As Mike had said, the place had once been an inn and still bore traces of such. And here the three men could see light coming from both the stable and the main structure. None were in a hurry, however, to jump down from their carriage.

"I don't know," Wollcott said, shaking his head, "I don't like the looks of this place."

"I agree," Halliwell said emphatically. "I vote we go back to the inn and return in the morning. Even if he is here Randall must be fast asleep or he'd have been outside by now to welcome us."

"Hmm, I admit the place is not prepossessing," Langley said. "Still, I think we ought to at least make a push to see if Randall is here. Otherwise we might have a wasted trip in the morning. If he's not here I say we should just go back to Brighton."

"A wise decision," Mike said sagely. "Would 'ee like me to hold the horses for 'ee while 'ee knock at the door?"

Langley looked at the fellow witheringly. After a moment he said, "I suppose we have no choice unless one of you wants to stay with them."

Halliwell spoke up at once. "I will. If Randall really is here, then I'll climb down, but I'm dashed if I'll do so otherwise."

Mike shrugged and clumsily got down to the ground. "As 'ee wish, sir. This way, gen'lemun," he said to Langley and Wollcott as he led the way to the back door.

He did, however, step aside to allow Langley to rap on the wooden door. It was opened at once by an immaculately dressed Frenchman who bowed low and said, "Ah, how delightful to see you, Major Langley. And Captain Wollcott. Your friend, Captain Carswell, is impatient to see you, I've no doubt."

Langley hesitated. "How the devil do you know my name?" he demanded.

The Frenchman permitted himself a small laugh. "Why, gentlemen, I assure you that you, Major Langley, and Captain Wollcott, have been described to me in terms that make you quite unmistakeable." He paused, leaned out the door to look for their carriage and spied Halliwell in it. "Won't you invite your other friend, whoever he may be, to join us?" he asked.

"Do you mean to say Carswell didn't describe Halliwell to you as well?" Wollcott muttered with sarcasm.

Langley ignored him, however, and turned and called out, "Freddy! Come down and join us. This fellow says Randall is here and eager to see us."

With a coarse oath that it was perhaps as well they could not hear clearly, the Viscount Halliwell climbed down from the carriage. Reins in hand he called out, "What do I do with the horses?"

Mike, sounding considerably more sober now, said, "I'll see to the 'orses, sir."

Halliwell waited until the fellow reached him and took charge of the reins before he joined his friends in the doorway of the cottage. Then, impatience evident in his voice, he said, "Well, where is Carswell?"

"Right this way, gentlemen, right this way," the Frenchman said with another low bow.

Exchanging perplexed glances, the three men followed their host to the head of some stairs. "Go down there?" Wollcott demanded. "Preposterous!"

With exaggerated innocence the Frenchman said, "But my dear sirs, that is where you will find your friend, I assure you."

A trifle roughly Langley turned to the other two and said, "Why don't you wait here? I shall go down and discover what sort of nonsense is afoot and then come back up and tell you. And if Randall has passed out drunk again, I'll never let him hear the end of it."

"Capital notion," Wollcott said heartily.

"Yes, indeed. I don't fancy going down those steps unless I absolutely must," Halliwell agreed grumpily.

From behind them a voice that held a great deal of menace said, "Ah, but I am afraid, gentlemen, that you absolutely must all go down there right now."

As one the three turned to find a second Frenchman and two burly Englishmen standing there. The Frenchman held a pistol in each hand and the two English fellows, one of them Mike, each held a stout stick. The Frenchman contrived to bow without taking either his eyes or his pistols off the three men. "I am desolate to have to distress you so quickly after your arrival, but I really must insist that you go down those stairs."

"And Carswell?" Wollcott demanded, breathing heavily. "I suppose that was just a ruse to get us here?"

"But no," the Frenchman replied with wide-eyed innocence. "I assure you he is down there. Come, see for yourself."

Instinctively, Halliwell and Wollcott turned to Langley for direction. With a sigh Anthony said, "I suppose we must do as we are bid. Unless either of you cares to have a bullet in your head. Somehow, I have the unhappy feeling our host is a dead shot."

The Frenchman smiled happily and bowed, once again not letting his alertness waver. "How delightful to deal with such a perceptive fellow as yourself, Major Langley. You will not doubt me, I am sure, when I say that unless you begin to descend those steps in one minute I shall be forced to put a bullet into one of you three anyway. A nonfatal bullet, of course, but painful nevertheless, I fear."

With a snort of disgust Langley turned and led the way. Halliwell and Wollcott followed quietly. At the bottom of the stairs they encountered a locked door, one that the first Frenchman hastened to open for them. Their next sight was of two figures seated at a table around which were two other empty chairs. Wollcott rushed forward.

"Randall! Are you all right? And who is this?"

"As well as can be expected," Carswell replied dully. "And this is my illegitimate cousin Jeremy."

The youth sulkily murmured some sort of greeting that left no one in doubt of his total disinterest in the new arrivals. Halliwell stepped forward. "Good lord, Randall, you never mentioned the lad before."

"That is because I had not made his acquaintance before," Carswell replied easily. "Which is why he still possesses such abominable manners. But I assure you he has satisfied me as to his credentials."

Now Langley stepped forward. "This is a bad business," he said, "not helped by the presence of a sorry gosling like your cousin. Randall, what the devil is going on here?"

From behind him the second Frenchman sighed, "Three of you. Why do you all persist in arriving with unexpected companions? I really cannot be expected to provide for so many."

"Then don't," Halliwell retorted cheerfully. "Let me go. Let us all go, for that matter, and you needn't provide for any of us."

Rather coldly the Frenchman replied, "I shall contrive. As for what is going on, well I can tell you that, although I shan't until morning. You are free, all of you, to speculate as much as you wish with Captain Carswell, though I cannot attest to the accuracy of his notions."

And with that the door was slammed behind them and locked, leaving the five in almost complete darkness. The only light came from the moon through the narrow window slits near the ceiling of the cellar. Fairly quickly their eyes adjusted to the situation. When the sound of footsteps had completely died away Langley asked again, this time more calmly, "What is going on, Randall?"

Carswell shrugged. "I wish I could tell you for certain," he said. "They abducted me and Jeremy as well. Drugged us and brought us here. And forced me to write that letter to you. They have some notion you've got secret papers or something that they wish to get hold of."

Langley answered grimly. "I wonder how they knew about the papers." To the others he explained, "I am carrying papers, secret papers, from Wellington to Prinny, in Brighton. Prinny was to look them over and give his approval to some of Wellington's plans, if I could persuade him to do so." He paused, then added with a rueful laugh, "Actually, I have to persuade Prinny since Wellington means to carry out those plans in any event. Anyway, after I succeeded, I was to return to Spain and report to Wellington."

"Good God, man, where are they now?" Wollcott demanded.

"In my baggage, upstairs," Langley replied bitterly.

Halliwell snorted in disbelief. "Poppycock! You haven't been acting like a man on a secret mission. You've dawdled about enjoying yourself and made no effort to arrange to return to the Continent."

"That was on purpose," Langley said witheringly. "No one was supposed to guess that I was here for that reason. No one was meant to guess that Wellington proposed a new offensive. Boney's spies were to think everything was going as before. And I'm wondering if I made a mistake in trusting Carswell with the knowledge."

"Now wait a minute—" Carswell began when

the sound of footsteps hurrying up the stairs stopped all of them from speaking.

Halliwell groaned. "That's done it. Now they know precisely where to look for those papers, thanks to our stupidity."

"So they do," Carswell said thoughtfully, "so they do."

"I must say you're taking this demmed coolly," Halliwell said angrily. "Don't you realize what this means?"

Carswell didn't answer but Wollcott said, "It means that we had better do our best to break out of here and try to get those papers back. As I recall, Lullington isn't that far from the sea and a small boat could put in to collect those Frenchmen if it wanted to."

At this Carswell added, "He did say they had a boat standing offshore waiting for their signal at any time, day or night. Though I don't doubt they would prefer night."

"That settles it, we've got to get out," Wollcott repeated. "But how? Carswell, you've seen this place in daylight, what do you suggest?"

"What are you asking him for?" Halliwell demanded. "At this point I'm half convinced he's in league with them. Or his so-called cousin is. You said yourself, Tony, that he was the only one you told."

"But who did Prinny tell?" Wollcott said before the other two had a chance to reply. "We've known Randall a long time and personally I find it easier to believe that someone on Prinny's side of it gave away the game than that Randall did."

There was silence and then Langley said, "That's true enough. Who knows what Prinny said in his cups or his friends said in theirs."

"Sorry, Randall," Halliwell said gruffly. "For a moment there I just couldn't see any other explanation. But why the devil did you write the letter for them?"

From behind the door the second Frenchman's voice replied, startling all of them, "I can explain that. We threatened to torture his cousin and abduct the lot of you anyway. I don't doubt he thought you'd outwit us. Instead, you have generously given us all of the information we need to know. My friends have already found the papers, Major Langley. I really must advise you to take better care of them in the future. If you have a military future, that is. And now I am desolate but I must leave you. I have a voyage by sea to make tonight. Captain Carswell, I must ask you to come over to the door. Alone. You are coming with me. Please hurry or I shall be forced to put a bullet through every one of your friends."

Slowly, reluctantly, Carswell rose and painfully limped over to the door. "What about my cousin?" he asked roughly.

"He stays," was the reply.

"Then so do I," Carswell answered.

After a moment's silence the Frenchman said roughly, "Oh very well. Let him come along. But trouble from either of you and I shoot."

"Quickly, Jeremy," Carswell told his cousin, his voice brooking no argument.

Jeremy did as he was bid and the door opened to allow the two to leave the cellar prison. The Frenchman hastily relocked the door, then motioned to the pair. Solemnly they preceded him up the steps, Carswell leaning on Jeremy for support.

When the footsteps had died away and the

sound of a door above slammed shut, the three men broke into a round of curses. "Dash it all!" Wollcott exclaimed last. "That's twice they tricked us into thinking they had gone and left us alone. And we fell for it. Do you think there is anyone there now?"

16

OUT in the courtyard Perrin put away his pistol. As the other men saddled up horses he said to Carswell, "I shall bid you farewell here, captain, unless you really do wish to come with me. No? Somehow I thought not. A pity, you would like France. Well, should anyone discover the note you sent your friends, you need merely say that they never arrived. Or that they were lost in an unfortunate fire." He paused, then said, "I should prefer that it go unknown that we managed to acquire Major Langley's papers."

But Carswell's attention was caught by the word *fire*. "What is going to happen to them?" he asked roughly.

Perrin shrugged. "As I told you, they will be lost in an unfortunate fire. Such a terrible pity. You do not mean to try to stop me, I hope. It would be such a pity to have to kill you as well."

"Stop you?" Carswell retorted. "I hope to be long gone by then."

"I think not," Perrin said regretfully. "Oh, do not misunderstand. I have no intention that you should die in the fire. No, I simply mean to make

144

sure you cannot interfere with my plans. My men will shut you up in the old Lullington church. Tomorrow or the next day I am sure someone will find and release you. And the boy. It is just that I am a careful man, you see. The fire, even, will not start for some two hours, time for me to get away to the coast, just in case something should go wrong."

Carswell nodded and waited meekly until the two burly guards came over and said it was time to go. Then he and Jeremy followed them across the fields toward a clump of trees. As before, he leaned heavily upon Jeremy for support, going slowly because of his leg. "Sorry, lad, can you manage?" Carswell asked halfway there.

"Somehow," Jeremy replied curtly.

Their destination was a tiny church with a number of windows, giving the two hope of escape. When they were closer, however, it became clear that their guards meant to take no chances. One of the men produced a rope and bound their hands in front of them. Inside the church he tied the other end of the ropes to the church railing. "Someone'll find 'ee soon enough," Mike said, and then the two men left shutting the door behind them.

When they were gone Captain Carswell muttered to himself, "I did not bargain on this. I wonder how much time we have?"

"An hour or two, I should imagine. That's what the Frenchman said. That is, if you do mean to try to rescue your friends," Mary replied tightly. She paused, then added hopefully, "I don't suppose any of your skills extend to getting out of ropes?"

"I wish they did," Carswell said grimly. "I had taken the precaution of carrying a knife tucked in my boot, but they seem to have taken that. I checked while our hands were free in that cellar," he concluded almost apologetically.

In the darkness Carswell could see Mary start. "What is it?" he asked her anxiously.

With a wry grin the captain could not see Mary replied, "*I'm* a fool! Like you, I hid a knife in my boot, but unfortunately, I forgot to check for it before. I don't know if it is still there."

"Can't you feel it?" Carswell asked in disbelief.

It was Mary's turn to be apologetic. "It's a very small knife," she said. "But the only one I could obtain. Do you think if we shift around a bit you could manage to reach my boots and check for it for me?"

"Which boot?" Carswell asked grimly.

"The right one," Mary replied.

As they strained to get in position Carswell could not help but ask, "What the devil were you doing carrying a knife, anyway?"

Mary let out a sigh of exasperation. "I may be impulsive and naive, but I am not an idiot. If I ran into trouble, back in Brighton when I came looking for you, I wanted some way to defend myself."

Carswell, who by now had managed to extract the small knife from Mary's boot, said in disbelief, "And you thought this would do it? It's scarcely larger than a fruit knife!" Then, without a pause, he told her, "Hold out your hands. I'll try to cut your ropes first. I'd rather that than trust you to cut mine under these circumstances."

Mary did as she was bid, then said defensively, "A sharp thrust at the right moment might well have deterred an attacker. Or at least startled him so that I might get away. What would you have done in my place?"

"Stayed at home where I belonged," Carswell retorted sharply.

"To be sure," Mary said politely. "Had you been born a woman naturally you would have been the most demure creature alive."

Momentarily, Carswell paused in his efforts to cut the rope. With a quirky smile that Miss Farnham could not see he said, "No doubt. That or the wildest."

Mary laughed and Carswell went back to work on her bonds. Then, thoughtfully, she said, "I wonder why they left me my knife?"

Witheringly, Carswell replied, "Obviously they never bothered to search you thoroughly or they would have discovered your sex. Though even if they had searched you I am in doubt they could have found such a tiny thing as this unless they were looking for it."

"They found your knife," Mary pointed out.

"Mine was five times this size," Carswell retorted. Then, a little later, he gave a small cry of triumph and Mary's hands were free. Relinquishing the knife to her he said, "Here, now cut me free. For God's sake be careful. And hurry!"

Without a word, Mary did as she was bid. Or tried to, at any rate. After several minutes of almost fruitless effort she began to agree with Carswell's disdain of the knife. Eventually, however, she managed to cut through the ropes and he was unbound as well. A few minutes more sufficed to see them free of the church since it turned out the door lacked a lock. And they were headed back across the fields, crouched low, to their former prison.

It was then that Mary had her greatest shock yet. Not only did the captain not need to lean on her, but he moved almost as quickly as she could.

Noting her look of astonishment Carswell laughed and said, "I thought it might help if they under-estimated what I could do."

"Were you pretending in Ipswich as well?" Mary asked, a trifle bitterly.

Carswell shook his head. "No," he replied grimly, "for the past two weeks I have been doing everything I could to strengthen my leg. It appears to have worked, fortunately. Now come on, let's go!"

As they went, Carswell gave Mary instructions. "Stay low. We don't want anyone to see us. And when we get there, you stay behind while I check if anyone is still there. I don't want to have to worry about you as well as freeing my friends."

Mary kept her counsel. She had no intention of being a problem to the captain, but neither did she intend to stay back if he needed aid. It would not help his peace of mind however, she reflected, if he knew that, so she kept quiet and nodded whenever he looked at her.

Although everything seemed to have happened quickly, Carswell was alarmed at how much time had passed as reckoned by the night sky. Perrin and Dugard must have reached the coast by now and their henchmen would have orders to burn down the house as early as possible before anyone would be awake to see and try to put out the fire.

Carswell was right. The first tendrils of smoke rose toward the sky while they were still more than a long field away. Abandoning caution the captain began to run as quickly as he could with his one lame leg, calling over his shoulder, "Stay down and out of sight! I'll be back for you later."

By the time he reached the courtyard of the former inn it was evident that Perrin and Dugard's men had already made good their escape. They had first, however, doused the structure in something flammable for it was burning strongly. The situation might have been hopeless save for the fact that the men had set it to burn brightest at the end of the structure away from the cellar door. No doubt, Carswell thought grimly, out of fear that the door would burn down and free his friends before the heat and smoke could kill them. After all, they had not thought there was any danger of a rescue.

Whatever the reason, Carswell did not hesitate but entered the cottage and threw open the upper door of the cellar. Only then did he realize the lower one must be locked and he had no means to open it. Scarcely had he completed the thought when a figure appeared beside him, dripping wet, holding out an ax.

"I found it abandoned near the burning barn," Mary told him tersely.

He didn't wait to thank her but grabbed the ax and thrust her toward the outer door. Below, he could hear his friends shouting for help but let the sound of the ax answer for him. A few minutes later they were free, and all four headed up the steps toward the open outer door. Much of the ground floor was already ablaze and only desperation could have made the men throw themselves into the flames to reach the open doorway the fire guarded.

Outside, they landed atop one another and were rolling in the dirt to try to put out the flames that had caught on their clothing when suddenly one bucket of water and then another splashed over them. Langley was the first to recover. Looking up at the bedraggled figure standing nearby with two now-empty buckets on the ground beside him, Langley said, "Thank you, my boy. Randall, I begin to think I may have misjudged your poor cousin."

There was no time for anyone to reply, however, for they were still all too close to the burning buildings for comfort. Halliwell's horses and his carriage were gone, of course, so the five made their way on foot across the fields in the direction of the Lullington village inn.

As Wollcott said, without humor, "By the time we reach it on foot, it'll scarcely be too early to ask for some food and inquire about horses."

About this time Halliwell noticed just how bedraggled Carswell's cousin looked and he asked, "What the deuce happened to you, boy? Fall into a stream?"

With a voice they had to strain to hear, Jeremy replied nonchalantly, "Doused m'self with water. Didn't want to catch on fire."

"Good thinking," Wollcott said with patent admiration. "Shows sense, your cousin does, Randall."

A short grunt was Carswell's only reply. It was about this time that Langley commented, "You're managing quite well, I'd say, Randall, for a man with a bad leg."

Carswell grinned. "You should have seen me when Perrin and Dugard were around. You would have thought me an absolute cripple." After a moment he added cryptically, "They headed straight for the coast. Seaford, I'd guess. Aboard ship by now and headed for Boney. We did it."

A gasp from the boy drew everyone's attention to Jeremy. His eyes were large and round under the cap he had somehow managed not to lose, despite everything. In exasperation, Langley looked from Carswell to Jeremy and back again. Finally he said, his voice dangerously quiet, "Before we go any further, Randall, we've got to decide what to do about your cousin. I tell you frankly that I don't trust the boy and I think you're damn foolish if you do."

Carswell drew his brows together in a frown. "What is it that you suspect Jeremy of doing?" he asked.

"Working for those two Frenchmen," Langley replied curtly. "And just now we can't afford that."

Thoughtfully, Wollcott added, "He did appear just before they abducted you, Randall. Extremely convenient if they wanted to plant a spy."

"Me? A spy?" Jeremy blurted out in a high voice.

Carswell's frown deepened. "I assure you, Jeremy is not a spy," he said gravely.

"So you tell us, Randall," Halliwell replied quietly, ignoring his two companions' snorts of disbelief. "But I'm afraid you shall find us a trifle difficult to convince. Unless you can tell us more about your, er, cousin, of course. Otherwise, how can you be so certain about a lad you met less than two days ago?"

A hint of desperation appeared in Carswell's eyes and more than a hint in Jeremy's. "I've known the boy longer than that," the captain said quickly.

"What? But you told me you'd never laid eyes on him before when I brought him up to your rooms," Langley said with astonishment, "and the boy swore the same thing. Were you lying to me then?"

The morning light had begun to brighten the sky

for several minutes and Halliwell, who had been staring at the still wet boy, now said in a rather strangled voice, "Tony, I think he's telling you the truth. About knowing the boy, I mean. And I don't think he's a spy."

The other men turned to Halliwell in astonishment and then let their eyes follow his. In the ever brighter morning light and with the wet clothes clinging to her body, it was impossible for Mary to conceal that she was a woman.

"Good God!" Wollcott said.

"Do I know you?" Langley asked in a puzzled voice. "You look very familiar."

Halliwell sketched a short bow and said, still in a rather strangled voice, "Your servant, Miss Farnham. May I ask how you come to be here in this fantastic situation with us?"

Carswell stepped to Mary's side and put an arm around her shoulder as she began to shiver from the cold and everything else that had occurred. "Don't worry," he told her. "None of these fellows will betray you. Not one," he said, fixing each of his friends with a quelling look in turn, "will betray that you were in my company and dressed in these clothes."

" 'Course not," Halliwell said hastily.

"Won't say a word," Wollcott seconded.

"Of course we shan't," Langley agreed. "But I must say I should like to know how you happened to end up here with us, Miss Farnham."

Carswell gave them a rapid, rather edited version of events. When he was done, the four men looked at one another. "Now what?" Wollcott asked. "We can't simply walk into the inn with her. Someone is sure to realize she's a woman and then the fat will be in the fire."

"Not if we're in there only long enough to arrange for food and horses," Carswell said firmly. "You would be astonished to realize how well Miss Farnham can imitate a young man's swagger. Particularly if she does not speak."

"But how will we get her back into Brighton?" Langley demanded. "It's near dawn now and everyone will be sleepy and not inclined to notice much of anything. But it will be broad daylight by the time we get to Brighton. You must see, Randall, that we can't take Miss Farnham back dressed as a boy."

"I've thought of that," Carswell replied. "Between here and there we'll surely pass through a somewhat larger village and can purchase some suitable clothing, preferably a riding habit, for Miss Farnham. Then she can return alone and pretend she got lost." He paused and turned to Mary. "Is that all right with you? Or would you rather I came with you and explained to your Aunt Gwendolyn?"

"Lord no!" Mary exclaimed. "That would only make matters far worse. It would be better if I face them alone."

"By gad, the girl does have courage!" Wollcott exclaimed, prompting the others to laughter.

"Good, then let's go before the day grows any longer," Carswell said curtly.

17

IT was with great trepidation that Mary Farnham approached the back door of her aunt and uncle's Brighton residence. Captain Carswell and his companions had been unable to obtain any clothing, in the small towns they had passed through, suitable to her station. In fact, they had counted themselves fortunate that one innkeeper's wife had been in service before her recent marriage and was willing to part with the uniform she had then worn. So it was as a parlormaid, and a rather disheveled one at that, that Mary came to the back door. She had not really expected to be able to reach her room unseen; nevertheless, she could not help but feel distressed at the uproar her sudden appearance aroused.

The cook succumbed to spasms. The upstairs maid immediately knelt down to look after the cook. The downstairs maid dropped the tea tray she was carrying and the majordomo of the staff regarded Mary with a quelling stare as he said repressively, "I shall tell the master and mistress you have returned, Miss Farnham. If you would be so good as to wait a moment, I feel sure that one of the maids can show you up the back way to your room. You will not wish to greet your aunt and uncle in those clothes."

It was all Mary could do not to drop the fellow a curtsy. Instead, she remained quite still until he had gone and then assisted the upstairs maid in getting the cook into her comfortable chair before asking another maid, Sara, to take her upstairs. The back way, of course. They left the cook fanning herself and murmuring about apparitions while the poor downstairs maid continued to pick up the pieces of broken crockery from the tea tray. The girl was heard to mutter that it was most fortunate that certain people had chosen the end of tea time and not the beginning to arrive to startle poor folks out of their wits. A sentiment clearly shared by the other servants as well, judging by their vehement nods of agreement.

On that note Mary Farnham hastily ascended the back stairs and reached her room unseen by either her aunt, her uncle, or any of their afternoon callers. A circumstance for which she was devoutly grateful.

It was some time later, after a much needed bath, that Mary Farnham was called upon to face her aunt and uncle. The afternoon callers had gone, the servants were dismissed from the room, and Mary stood in the drawing room with her back to the unlit fireplace. Nervously she clenched and unclenched her fists in the folds of her skirt, a modish creation of sprigged muslin meant to both give her courage and forestall criticism of her appearance.

Taking pity on her niece, Gwendolyn said kindly, "Sit down, child, we shan't eat you."

"At any rate not until we are certain we have cause to," Hubert added grumpily. "Where have you been?"

"And why didn't you leave us a note?" Gwendolyn added gently. "Or tell us where you were going?"

"It's the theater, I collect. Or a man," Hubert said before Mary could answer. "I shall tell you beforehand that we already know Captain Carswell has also not been seen since day before yesterday."

"Night before yesterday," Mary corrected him gently, then colored as she realized what her words revealed.

Fixing his niece with a piercing stare Hubert Foster said, "Just so. Captain Carswell was it, then? Are we to expect him to call upon us? His intentions, I hope, are honorable, however improper his actions may have been."

Mary had gone pale now and Gwendolyn intervened. "Give the child a chance to answer," she said. "I collect there is more to this than a lovers' tryst."

Mary nodded. "Yes. But I cannot tell you what it was. That is not my secret to reveal. As for Captain Carswell, he said he would speak with you himself but his intentions . . . his intentions regarding me are, I should guess, nonexistent."

"*What?*" Hubert thundered. "You admit you spent the missing time in his company and yet tell me he has no intentions toward you? By God, I'll call the fellow out!"

"You can't," Gwendolyn told her husband calmly. "Dueling is illegal. A thrashing, on the other hand, might answer very well."

"No!" Mary cried. Then, a trifle desperately, she

said, "It wasn't like that! I went to see him. We were both abducted. We only managed to escape this morning. Nothing happened between us!"

Hubert regarded his niece with patent disbelief. "Abducted?" he said. "Here? In Brighton? Poppycock! There are footpads aplenty in London, but Brighton is safe enough. You are merely trying to protect the scoundrel."

"But it's true!" Miss Farnham told him.

"Mary," Gwendolyn addressed her niece gently, "I don't doubt you believe you were abducted. But perhaps you simply misunderstood the circumstances. Why don't you tell us who is supposed to have abducted you and where they took you?"

Abruptly, Mary turned her back on them. Over her shoulder she said roughly, "I can't. I told you, it's not my secret to tell."

Hubert would have said more but Gwendolyn forestalled him. She stood and put a comforting arm around Mary's shoulders. "There, there, child," she said gently. "I don't doubt you've had a rough time of it. Why don't you go up to bed, right now, and I'll have one of the maids bring you up a tray. Then you must try to sleep, for you look all tired out. Time enough tomorrow to sort all of this through."

Impulsively, Mary gave her aunt a hug and nodded. She even managed a tremulous smile. Then, with a curtsy to her uncle, she left them to go to her room. When she was gone Hubert addressed his wife anxiously. "Do you think the poor girl has gone round the edge? Lost her wits, I mean?"

Gwendolyn took some time before she replied, "No, I don't think so. I don't know what occurred and it is clear to me the poor child's nerves are overset, but she has not lost her wits. I think you had best have a word with Captain Carswell and see what he has to say about all of this."

"Right," Hubert said, and heaved himself to his feet. "I'll go round to his hotel straightaway."

He started for the door but Gwendolyn stopped him. "No, I don't think so," she said slowly as she took his arm affectionately. "If you go round tonight, word will get about and it will be noticed that neither he nor our niece was seen for the past two days and that as soon as he reappeared you were on his doorstep to speak to him. Someone is sure to remark upon it. Wait until tomorrow and see if you can contrive to meet him as if by chance. There will be an assembly at the Castle Inn and perhaps you may see him then."

"A good notion, my love," Hubert said, giving his wife an affectionate kiss upon her forehead. "A good thing you've such a wise head upon your shoulders for I confess to being so angry with Carswell that I should not have had the patience to think it through. Do you think we'll be obliged to have the fellow as a nephew-in-law?"

Gwendolyn shrugged. "I don't know. You heard Mary say she thought he had no romantic intentions toward her, and I suppose she must know. But I confess none of this makes any sense to me. I only hope the captain will tell you more. I shouldn't like to think that at any moment Mary might disappear again and leave us all anxious for her."

In a small tavern just outside of Brighton, the four men, Langley, Carswell, Wollcott, and Halliwell, sat discussing what had occurred. "What do you do next?" Carswell asked curtly.

"Make our way back to Wellington's camp," Langley replied, just as curtly.

"Very quietly," Wollcott added. "We shan't want to draw attention to ourselves, after all."

"Your things?" Carswell persisted.

"Halliwell can collect them," Langley answered after a moment.

"Risky?" Carswell suggested.

Langley shook his head. "No one has been paying much attention to Freddy. After all, Perrin didn't know who he was. We mentioned his name but I doubt the Frenchmen cared."

"Besides," Halliwell added, looking at his impeccably shined boot thoughtfully, "I should rather enjoy encountering someone who had the audacity to question me. I don't think the fellow would be inclined to gossip afterward."

Wollcott laughed appreciatively. "I do believe Freddy is regretting having sold out his colors."

"Me?" Halliwell raised an eyebrow disdainfully. "On the contrary, I am enjoying the life of a viscount immensely. It just becomes a trifle boring from time to time," he added wistfully.

Again Wollcott laughed and the others joined him. After a moment, however, Langley turned to Carswell and said seriously, "What will you do, Randall?"

"Return to my quarters, of course, that will be expected," Carswell replied thoughtfully. "Drink a trifle too much, as though something is preying on my mind, but never in the disreputable places where I met Perrin and Dugard. If I am asked about you I shall be damned evasive and we shall see what presents itself."

Langley nodded. "And Miss Farnham? Will she have the sense to keep her mouth shut?"

"I think so," Carswell said with an odd smile.

"Well I, for one, cannot like having a young chit involved," Wollcott said reprovingly. "A girl who would behave so outrageously as to dress up as a young man is even worse. How do we know what Miss Farnham will do next? Perhaps she is unbalanced or wants to be notorious or something. Certainly no young lady I know would do such a thing!"

Again Carswell smiled but his words were sober as he replied, "Miss Farnham is neither unbalanced nor desires notoriety, I assure you."

"So you say," Wollcott snorted. "But then you brought her into this mess in the first place."

Slowly, Carswell rose to his feet. "I do say so," he told his friends amiably, looking down at them. "More than that, anyone who questions Miss Farnham's qualities or gossips about what has occurred shall have to answer to me." He hesitated, then added, "Her circumstances are her own affair and I shall not repeat what I know of them. But I will say that any one of us, in her position, might well have acted the same and had to develop skills as unconventional as, perhaps, playing the part of a boy."

"Oh, do sit down," Halliwell said impatiently. "Honestly! Glaring at us as though we were your worst enemies instead of your friends! Jack was only voicing what anyone might think. But if you vouch for the girl, why then you must know we shall take you at your word and no more shall be said about the matter."

"Yes, do sit down, you nodcock," Wollcott added goodnaturedly. "None of us is foolish enough to take on a fellow in your evidently besotted condition. If you've fallen in love, that's your affair. Besides, I will say that I was impressed with your Miss Farnham today. No megrims, no vapors, just good common sense. I should give a lot to find another young lady who would go through a day and night like yesterday and not spend the next week berating me for it," he added hastily as a dangerous gleam appeared in Carswell's eye.

The captain nodded curtly. "We could have used a few more men with as sound a head in the peninsula," he said. "At any rate, enough of Miss Farnham. I'd best be off to Brighton and you'd best be on your way. Do you catch a boat from the coast or go through London?" he asked Langley and Wollcott.

Langley tipped back his chair and took a moment before he replied slowly, "I don't think you want to know that, Randall. This way, should anyone ask you what became of us, you can honestly say that you don't know where we are or what we are doing."

The four men shared another brief laugh, then rose from their chairs and went outside to their horses. All but Halliwell. He bid his friends good-bye but then went back inside, prepared to spend a rather uncomfortable night at the tavern. "I'll not return to Brighton until tomorrow," he explained. "And if anyone asks, I shall merely smile grimly and say that I had something of an adventure but don't wish to talk about it."

18

ALTHOUGH Mary Farnham did not dislike assemblies, she looked forward to the next night's dance with some trepidation. No one could have known of her adventure and she had her Aunt Gwendolyn's word that her disappearance had been kept from everyone. And yet Mary could not help but feel that they must know what she had done. As for her aunt and uncle, nothing could have exceeded their kindness in forbearing to quiz her, or their gentleness in general. Almost, Mary thought wryly, as though they thought she might break with rough handling. Which, given the bizarre events of the past two days and her refusal to explain any of it, was understandable.

The other cause for her reluctance to attend the assembly was that Mary fully expected Captain Carswell would be there. Although he could not dance, he had made it his habit to attend the Brighton assemblies and converse with acquaintances and with young ladies temporarily without partners as well as with the many officers who were always to be found there.

Still, it was impossible to refuse to go. Particularly when her Aunt Gwendolyn fixed her with a kind but firm stare and said quietly, "I have put it about that you were ill. It is imperative, however, that you now present yourself, otherwise I cannot answer for the gossip that might arise."

Which later, in view of that night's events, was to be remembered by Mary as an exquisitely ironic thing to say. Still, at the time it made sense.

In any event, promptly at the hour appointed by her aunt, Mary Farnham descended the stairs of the Brighton residence dressed in a pale blue satin and lace confection designed by Gwendolyn Foster's favorite modiste. Somewhat to her astonishment she discovered that her Uncle Hubert but not her aunt was to accompany her to the assembly. When she tried to protest, Aunt Gwendolyn kissed her cheek and said, "Nonsense! You look delightful, Mary. As for me, reluctant though I am to admit it, I am beginning to show and cannot go out in my dancing dress tonight. Besides, I find myself rather fatigued and the doctor has forbidden such activities for a few days at the very least."

"But when did this happen?" Mary asked with remorse. "It—it wasn't because I ran away, was it?"

Gwendolyn shook her head but Hubert intervened. Sternly, he told his niece, "Yes, it was. Or at any rate the doctor said that Gwen must not be subjected to any distress or exertion for the next week or two and then we shall see how she is. And if you hadn't spent the day in your room, avoiding us, you would have known that the doctor had been called."

"I'm so sorry," Mary said, a stricken look upon her face.

At the sight of her distress, Hubert relented and, patting her shoulder, said, "Well, there now enough of that. To be sure we were both greatly distressed by your disappearance, but there is no saying that Gwen would not have had this trouble anyway. And the doctor is not unduly alarmed, he simply wishes Gwen to take every care of herself. Now come along, my child, before you give her the megrims with that Friday face of yours. I shall take you to the assembly and you will have a good time, I'll stand warrant for it!"

In the face of that there was nothing more to be said and Mary meekly did as she was bid.

They arrived at the assembly well after it had begun. Hubert lost no time in introducing Mary to those of his or Gwendolyn's acquaintances that she did not already know and very soon she was dancing with the son of one of those acquaintances. Everyone was quite kind, inquiring about her brief illness and expressing pleasure in seeing her again.

Mary was watching for him so she noticed when Carswell arrived. With a wry smile that startled her dancing partner she realized he once more was relying heavily upon his cane. If he saw her, however, he gave no evidence of it and not once did his eyes stray in her direction. So intent was Miss Farnham on observing Captain Carswell that a short time later, she entirely failed to notice the appearance of the Marquess of Alnwick.

The marquess, however, noticed Captain Carswell. He fixed the fellow with a malevolent stare and then elaborately turned his attention elsewhere. In the course of the next half hour he acquired a great deal of interesting information about the captain, including the circumstances of his arrival in Brighton. It is perhaps not surprising, therefore, that he was such an interested observer of Mary Farnham's encounter with the captain. An encounter that was brought about by her Uncle Hubert.

Hubert Foster asked his niece to dance, surprising in itself, and contrived to maneuver them so that they were quite near the captain when the dance ended. He then greeted Carswell with every evidence of goodwill. "Captain Carswell, my boy," he said with hearty amiability, "how are you?"

The captain cocked an eyebrow at Mary, but she merely shrugged her shoulders the tiniest bit. With a bow Carswell replied, "Your servant, Mr. Foster. I am very well. And yourself?"

"Fine, fine," Hubert replied heartily. "But we don't see nearly enough of you, my boy. M'wife Gwendolyn was saying so, just yesterday. Why don't you come round and pay us a call tomorrow?"

Carswell's eyebrows rose higher and Mary colored more deeply. Neither knew what to say but in any event a voice forestalled them. With icy politeness the gentleman said, "Perhaps the good captain has tired of his, er, provincial rose." To Mary he added coolly, "You are the provincial rose, are you not, ma'am? A pity. Perhaps if you had stayed in Ipswich you would have his interest still."

"What the devil are you talking about, Alnwick?" Hubert demanded.

The marquess picked an invisible speck of dust from his sleeve before he deigned to answer. "Why only that when I last saw Captain Carswell and this young lady they were dallying together in a town called Ipswich. A few weeks ago. I forget the particulars," he concluded with a careless wave of his hand.

"You mean when the captain was so good as to escort my niece from her home here in Brighton," Hubert retorted with equally icy politeness.

"Was that the story?" the marquess murmured. "How very clever of you!"

Mary felt her heart sink as she noticed the curious looks and the whispered conversations going on about them as the story spread. One or two ladies were already regarding her with malicious smiles and two of her earlier dancing partners hastily looked away, faces red, as she happened to catch their eyes. So distracted was she that she almost missed the first words of Carswell's reply.

"Indeed, I recall that encounter as well as you do," Carswell said with a bored yawn. Then, in a voice that turned suddenly harsh he went on, "Do you always, Lord Alnwick, force your attentions on unwilling young ladies, as you tried to do with my fiancée?"

Hubert Foster, who had started to turn toward the marquess in anger, abruptly halted and stared at the captain. Mary murmured something, her face now utterly pale. Even the marquess seemed startled as he said, "Fiancée? You are engaged to the young lady?"

Smoothly, Carswell took Mary's hand and drew her to his side. "A private engagement, to be sure," he said coolly. "One of long standing and known only to her family. I do not choose to rush my fences, you see, and have been waiting for her to come of age."

"Come of age?" Lord Alnwick objected. "She is scarcely a schoolroom miss."

"Some young ladies mature earlier than others," Carswell replied, ignoring the incensed look Mary turned on him.

"Nevertheless, that does not explain your presence unattended in Ipswich with the young lady," the marquess said silkily with narrowed eyes.

Carswell drew Mary even closer. His voice was still cool, however, as he replied, with raised eyebrows, "My dear marquess, I do not choose to explain anything to anyone. If you have a quarrel with that, why then call me out. I shall be delighted to meet you."

The marquess bowed. "On the contrary," he said smoothly, "I offer you my felicitations. And my apologies that I mistook the situation."

There was a gasp of breath from somewhere and the word coward might have been heard. Amused, the Marquess of Alnwick looked about him and raised a quizzing glass to his eye. Loudly enough for everyone nearby to hear he said, "Indeed, and why not? I have not reached the age of eight and forty by living a life of recklessness. Why should I fight a duel with this man over a young lady I have not the slightest interest in? Let other men be so foolish as to kill one another. The more ladies that will be left bereft for me to console!"

There was a ripple of laughter at the reply and the marquess calmly sauntered away. That left room for acquaintances of the Fosters to crowd around and ask Hubert if it were true that Mary was engaged to Carswell.

Hubert Foster looked from his niece to the captain and back again. Then, with what might have been a shrug he replied, "It is not my place to make such a confirmation, of course. That should come from her mother or stepfather. Or an official notice in the papers."

"Yes, but is it true?" Lady Crane persisted with exasperation.

"Or is there another explanation to this affair?" Lord Crane chimed in heavily.

Cornered, Hubert could only throw up his hands and turn to Carswell. "Well, my boy?" he asked, avoiding his niece's eyes. "Are you prepared to send an official notice to the papers yet, or shall I deny it all?"

Gravely, Carswell replied, "The notice will be sent off straightaway in the morning, sir. And I apologize that my reluctance to do so before has placed you in such an awkward position."

That pronouncement led to gratified murmurs and both Hubert and Mary were forced to endure the congratulations of a great many people before they were able to escape. Finally, when the last person had come up to them, Hubert turned to Mary and Carswell and said, in a voice that carried, "Well, well, it is getting late and I should like to take you home now, Mary. I am a trifle concerned about Gwendolyn. Do you mind?"

"Of course not," she said hastily.

Then, as though it had been an afterthought, Hubert asked Carswell, "I say, care to accompany us, captain? Gwendolyn won't mind seeing you tonight. No doubt she will wish to know all about what has occurred and she will want to hear it directly from you."

"I should like to tell her," Carswell replied gravely.

No more was said between the three as they took their leave of friends and made their way outside to where a carriage could be summoned. Once inside, Hubert turned to the captain and demanded, "What did you mean by saying you were engaged to my niece?"

Carswell's face remained quite impassive, but his eyes began to dance as he said, "Why, I thought that would be less vulgar than saying we were about to be leg-shackled or become tenant-for-life with one another, sir."

Fixing the younger man with a malevolent stare, Foster said, "That was not what I meant and you know it. What are we to do when no such formal notice is forthcoming? Say that you or my niece were so capricious as to break it off, after all? That will scarcely avert any scandal. Not when you've taken care to tell practically all of Brighton that the engagement is one of long standing and insulted the Marquess of Alnwick into the bargain."

"I'm sorry, was he a friend of yours?" Carswell asked sympathetically.

"No, he is not a friend of mine!" Hubert retorted explosively. "He is a damned poor fellow to make an enemy of, that's what! By tomorrow, anyone unfortunate enough to have missed today's assembly will still have heard the news of Mary's supposed engagement through his efforts. By Monday, all of London will know, I don't doubt. I repeat, what are we supposed to do when a formal notice of this suppposed engagement is not forthcoming?"

Captain Carswell regarded his nails intently before he replied, "Alnwick and I were already enemies. In any event, what makes you think the announcement will not be forthcoming? I fully expect it to be in the papers by the early part of the week, if not sooner."

Beside him Mary gasped. Carswell turned to her, took her hand, and raised it to his lips. Gravely he said, "Is something wrong, my dear?"

Mary's heart seemed to her to be beating wildly

and it was all she could do to answer, almost incoherently, "But you don't want. . . . I don't understand why. . . . You are roasting. . . . What will your family. . . . Uncle Hubert?"

The last two words were a plea for help, one that Hubert Foster understood very well. With a sigh he said, "A carriage, even a closed one such as this, is no place to discuss this matter. Carswell, when we get to my house you may have fifteen minutes alone with my niece to straighten this out while I check on my Gwendolyn and tell her what has occurred. Then I shall come back downstairs and expect some answers from you. This time without any nonsense."

"Of course," Carswell replied gravely.

"Of course?" Mary repeated in exasperation. "You say it as though it were the easiest thing in the world!"

"It is," he replied with a half smile.

"Oh to be sure," Mary said tartly. "You make a public announcement of an engagement I have no knowledge of and which you cannot know I will agree to, right after a disappearance you must know my uncle will wish to know about, and you calmly say you have all the answers my uncle could wish."

"Well, not quite all the answers," Carswell said apologetically. "Nor did I guarantee he would like them. But what are you in a dither about, my dear? You wanted to be an actress, didn't you? Well tonight I gave you another opportunity to act; to play the part of my fiancée."

"Act!" Mary all but shouted the word. "You are the one who ought to have been an actor. How could you say such nonsense? And in front of everyone my aunt and uncle know?"

"Children," Hubert's quietly spoken word cut through their argument and reduced the pair to silence. "That's better," he went on after a moment. "I said we would discuss this at my house. After all, I should not care to have to rely on the discretion of a coachman, would you?"

And that kept the pair silent for the rest of the short ride to the Foster household. Except for the one occasion when Carswell ventured to observe, "I like you in blue, Mary."

Her angry glare, however, effectively discouraged any other compliments he may have had in mind to make.

19

TRUE to his word, Hubert Foster left Captain Carswell and Mary alone in the drawing room while he went upstairs to see his wife. And to prepare her for the shock he felt sure would be forthcoming.

When they were alone Carswell turned to Mary, who regarded him with something of a hunted look in her eyes. Again he possessed himself of her hand and kissed it before he said, "I have distressed you, Mary. Will you tell me why?"

"Why?" she cried in disbelief, snatching her hand away from him. "You announce a sham engagement, in public, taking care to offend the one man who would most like to embarrass us, and you ask me why I am distressed?"

"But I thought you liked me," Carswell protested, his face the picture of innocence. "Is the thought of being betrothed to me so dreadful after all?"

Mary colored. "It is the thought of having to pretend to be betrothed to you I cannot like," she replied.

"But I thought you wanted to be an actress," he continued to protest.

Abruptly, Mary turned her back on him. Over her shoulder she said, "Not for something like this. Indeed, Captain Carswell, the past few days have cured me, I think of ever wanting to be an actress again."

There was no reply until the captain came closer and placed his hands gently on her shoulders, his cane once more discarded. He turned her around, tilted up her chin so she would look at him, and said with all seriousness, "And what if I said I did not mean the betrothal to be a sham? What if I said I was fully prepared to marry you?"

For a moment Mary Farnham swayed toward the captain, drawn by his warm, dark eyes. Then, suddenly, she pulled herself free. "No!" she said with a tiny cry.

"No?" he repeated curiously.

"I don't really know you," Mary protested.

Carswell crossed his arms over his chest. "And what is it you wish to know?" he asked evenly.

Mary twisted her hands together. "Wh-what about the past few days?" she demanded. "What happened with your friends. You betrayed them to those Frenchmen. No, I had forgotten. Major Langley seemed to know what you were doing. Perhaps you only betrayed your country. But can you understand that I want to know why?"

Carswell again placed his hands on her shoulders. Looking down into her face he said, "I cannot tell you now what that was about, Mary. Won't you trust me? Believe me when I tell you it was not what it seemed? I promise that before I force you to the altar I will tell you everything."

"No," Mary repeated, and once more pulled free of him. "I won't marry you." When she saw that Carswell's face darkened and his eyes took on a shuttered look she held out a hand toward him, in spite of herself. "Please understand," she said pleadingly, "I cannot let you do this. I know you can only be trying to marry me because you think you must. Because the Marquess of Alnwick has threatened my reputation. But I cannot let you marry me for a reason such as that."

At her words, Carswell's look lightened and a tiny smile crinkled the corner of his mouth as he said wryly, "No? Perhaps I was thinking of my own reputation. Won't you help me salvage that?"

"Don't jest about a thing like this," Mary said in exasperation.

Carswell came steadily toward Mary and she hastily backed away until she found herself against the wall looking up at him. Only then did he speak, the smile still playing at the corner of his mouth. "And if I said that I wanted to marry you?" he asked. "Not because I had to but because I found I could not do without you?"

As he spoke Carswell bent to kiss her lightly on the lips. To Mary, it seemed as though fire coursed through her at his touch. A trifle breathlessly she said, "You cannot mean it."

"And why not, my love?" he asked with the same wry smile, kissing her again.

Mary looked away. "You know me far too well to think you could want to wed me," she said, bitterness tinging her voice. "I am no demure young lady. You know about my stepbrother and you know about my recent escapades. Both as a boy and as a would-be actress. I cannot believe you wish to marry me after that."

With an oath Carswell pulled her to him and kissed her passionately on the lips as his arms tightened about her waist and back. "Mary, Mary!" he said in exasperation. "How could you

think those things would turn me against you?"
Then, with an effort, he put her away from him
and ran a hand roughly through his hair. "I am no
callow youth," he told her. "unable to believe in
anything except the dictates of the *ton*. We are a
pair, you and I, doing what we must, living each
day with a sense of what is real, not lost in some
fantasy world created by our peers. I don't want
some demure chit who can sew and paint and play
upon the pianoforte but is without two thoughts to
rub together in her head. Or worse, some clinging
vine who will expect me to think and make
decisions and have opinions for the both of us. I
want a woman just like you."

Once more Mary swayed toward him, wanting
desperately to believe the captain's words. Her
uncle's cold voice, however, was like a bucket of
cold water thrown over the pair of them. "Very
prettily said," Hubert Foster observed, closing the
drawing room door behind him and coming
forward into the room. "Mary, your Aunt
Gwendolyn would like to speak with you and I
should like to speak to Captain Carswell. I should
wait until after that, child, before I made any
plans. There are certain matters on which he has
yet to satisfy me and you have yet to satisfy your
aunt."

He spoke sternly and Mary could do no more
than curtsy to her uncle and go upstairs, with a
last pleading look at Carswell. He smiled
reassuringly at her but inside was far from feeling
so himself.

"I see you are managing very well without your
cane," Foster observed dryly.

"From time to time my leg improves a bit,"
Carswell agreed mildly.

Foster gave him a long, hard stare, then said sternly, "Sit down, Carswell. First of all, I should like to know what happened during those hours my niece was away from here. Secondly, if you are indeed serious about this betrothal I shall want to hear what you consider your prospects to be. It is my information that you are the younger son and that your father has more than once threatened to cut you off without a penny. That indeed your current allowance is dependent upon your not returning home. Not a very estimable situation for a gentleman considering matrimony."

"Quite true," Carswell agreed quietly. "My father and I have never gotten along well. That is one reason he bought me my colors. As for my prospects, I have not yet had time to think that through. I did not expect, you see, to be announcing my betrothal tonight," he added with an apologetic smile. "Indeed, I had not expected to announce my betrothal to Miss Farnham at all. However warm my feelings toward her may be, I have heretofore considered myself quite ineligible as a suitor. Perhaps you will say that I still am. But I could think of no other alternative when the Marquess of Alnwick told everyone about Ipswich."

"Quite," Hubert replied nodding curtly. "And under some circumstances your prospects would not matter. I believe you are in love with my niece and I do not think you a fortune hunter. But there are complications and you had better know something of my niece's own prospects."

Carswell frowned. "I understand her father left her very well provided for. Something in the nature of several thousand pounds a year, perhaps almost ten thousand."

Hubert Foster sighed heavily. "What I am about to tell you, Captain Carswell, is in the strictest confidence and I do not want my niece or anyone else to know. I wish to God I did not even have to tell you. Mary's father did leave such a trust fund for her. Unfortunately, her stepfather was the primary trustee. William Farnham never did know anything about human nature and in this case he made a particularly disastrous choice. Because of something Mary said when she first came to stay with us, I have made certain inquiries through my solicitor. I am afraid, Captain Carswell, that over the past eighteen months Mary's stepfather has systematically been taking money from the trust fund and putting it to his own account. At this point there is scarcely enough to provide her with a thousand pounds a year. Not poverty, but not what she ought to be accustomed to, either."

He paused. Carswell's face was dark with anger. "Will you call him to account for it?" he demanded harshly.

Hubert sighed heavily again. "I have already directed my solicitor to approach him discreetly with a letter from me telling him that I know what has occurred. But other inquiries I have made warn me that it is unlikely he will be able to cover the amount he has stolen. It seems the fellow has a taste for what he cannot afford, including gambling, at which he is notoriously unlucky. And a year and a half ago he had a particularly disastrous run of losses."

Carswell rose and paced the room. "I see," he said. "And I still wish to marry your niece. But I can understand your concern that I be able to provide for both of us since she cannot." He paused and looked directly at Hubert Foster as he added, "I hope you will believe that I do not wish she would, sir."

Foster held up a hand. "Peace, Carswell. I acquit you of being a fortune hunter, I have already said so. But you must see it is a concern I cannot ignore. The other is what occurred the past few days. Will you tell me?"

Carswell looked at his host as though weighing him up, then came abruptly to a decision. "Very well," he said. "I must, however, swear you to discretion as you did me. I will tell you what I can, and perhaps you will even be able to help me."

Mary was finding her interview with Gwendolyn Foster no easier to handle. In her quiet, well-bred voice Gwendolyn asked, "Are you very sure in your own mind, Mary, of Captain Carswell's character? Do you have no reservations as to his behavior toward you? And his intentions? I presume you have told him your expectations of the trust your father left for you?" Mary nodded and her aunt went on, "Has he been equally honest as to his lack of expectations?"

"We have not spoken of it," Mary replied. "Until tonight the subject of marriage between us seemed absurd."

Gwendolyn Foster continued to regard her niece steadily and after a moment Mary said, with a hint of desperation in her voice, "Surely Uncle Hubert has told you what occurred at the assembly? Surely you will agree that for the sake of my reputation I must be betrothed to Captain Carswell?"

Gently, Gwendolyn answered, "Hubert has told me. But I do not agree that is the only answer. Soon I shall be retiring to the country with Hubert to wait for the baby's birth. You could come with me. Perhaps you will meet someone there. Mary, I cannot promise this will be forgotten. I do know, however, that I cannot stand by while you perhaps make as great a mistake as your mother. I would rather see you stay unwed."

"I thought you liked Randall!" Mary protested.

"I did," Gwendolyn agreed. "I thought him a good, steadying influence on you but that did not mean I ever thought to see him wed to you. Mary, if we can bring you about there will be many gentlemen with far better expectations than Captain Carswell."

Bitterly Mary said, "I see. You are like all the other matchmaking ladies of the *ton*. All you can think of are titles and money and expectations, and feelings have no part in the occasion. I suppose you believe that a *tendre* for someone is vulgar and everyone rubs along together far better if there is only a mild respect between the pair although in a pinch even mere tolerance will do."

Gwendolyn laughed, then said with a shake of her head, "Now that is doing it much too brown, Mary. You have only to look at Hubert and myself to see that there is more than tolerance or even merely respect between us. I understand too well the importance of feelings. I only ask that you also understand the importance of using your head as well. The man who captures only our hearts and not our respect may not be the best choice to wed. That is why I ask you to think long and hard about your Captain Carswell before you tell me you are certain you want this match. All other considerations stand second to those, the heart and the head. Now come, admit I am no ogre but only someone who wishes the best for you."

Mary hugged her aunt. "I do know it," she said. "It is just that I am in such a whirl and I was hoping the answer could be as easy as just saying yes when Randall announced we were betrothed."

Again Gwendolyn laughed, but this time gently. "A choice that will affect the rest of your life and you expect it to be easy?" she chided her niece. "Impossible! But come, tell me the good things and the bad about your Captain Carswell and perhaps the questions will answer themselves."

Mary took her time before she said, "He knows me," she said slowly, "perhaps better than anyone else ever has. And he still tells me he wants to be married to me. He is not shocked by who I am and if I marry him I need never play a part, need never pretend to a conventional propriety that will never come with ease to me."

"That is no small thing," Gwendolyn agreed. "What else?"

"When I am with him I want to be better than myself," Mary went on, feeling her way. "To improve all the good things about myself and weed out the weak or foolish. I am not afraid he would ever try to make some sort of doll of me, all show and no substance, but rather I feel. . . . with him I shall always be trying to grow. Do you understand what I mean?"

"Far better than you might think," Gwendolyn agreed gravely. "And again I admit that these are important considerations. But I also ask you again, what do you know of his character? I must tell you that I am disturbed that he has sworn you to silence over your disappearance and that he did not immediately bring you back."

Quietly Mary replied, "He would have brought me back here if he could have."

Gwendolyn sighed, recognizing the look of obstinacy in her niece's eyes. "Very well, I shan't press you further. I only ask that you think long and hard about these questions in your own mind and if you have doubts, press Captain Carswell for answers before, not after, you are betrothed." She hesitated, then added, "And Mary, if we ask you to think about Captain Carswell's expectations it is not because we are mercenary. We ask only because it is a difficult thing to find oneself penniless."

Mary laughed gaily. "Now that is the one fear we do not have," she said. "We know my father left me well provided for!"

Gwendolyn started to speak, then changed her mind and only pressed her lips together in a forced smile.

20

THE Marquess of Alnwick was not a man who fought duels. He was known, however, as a man who never forgot grudges or allowed others to offend him unscathed. He had noted the astonishment with which Miss Farnham heard Captain Carswell announce their betrothal, and the distaste with which her uncle had reacted as well.

Further, he knew that word had it the captain had left the Foster household the night before and not in good spirits, had found a place to drink, and proceeded to put himself four sheets to the wind. Nor had he yet sent the expected notices to the papers. No messages of any sort had been sent by Carswell at all the entire next day. This led the marquess to smile grimly at his own image in the looking glass as he dressed for dinner at the Pavilion. He had already done his best to spread the tale of the supposed engagement, but now it looked as if there was further opportunity for mischief. With a laugh to himself the marquess summoned his secretary and told the fellow, "I wish you to send a notice to all the papers."

"Very good, m'lord, what sort of notice," the foppish young fellow asked.

"A notice of the betrothal of Captain Randall Carswell to Miss Mary Farnham. And oh yes, you are to sign his name to the notice," Alnwick said with a negligent wave of his hand.

The secretary, who had been hired for his willingness to accomplish the most extraordinary of tasks without surprise, merely asked quetly, "I collect the captain is unable to send the notice himself?"

The Marquess of Alnwick laughed humorlessly. "Let us rather say that the captain is reluctant to send the required notice and we are assisting him to do the honorable thing. Do you know, Martins, I greatly regret that I shall not be in Brighton to see their faces when they discover my assistance. I must send them notes of felicitation and ask when the wedding is to be."

Martins smiled grimly, himself the source of much of the marquess's information. "Particularly as word has it the captain had been barred from the Foster household until after last night's dance."

The marquess raised an eyebrow. "Had he indeed," he asked in a voice that sounded pleased. "Can it be that the young lady's family is not delighted at the prospect of Captain Carswell's entrance into their ranks? Dear, dear, I do wish we were not going to miss it all. However, I have a high regard for my health and something tells me it will be far healthier for me to be elsewhere when the news breaks. Ah, well, such is life. But that does remind me, I must make sure to have a private chat with Prinny tonight, and express to him my concern that the captain may have been trifling with the chit. He, I am sure, will be able to persuade the reluctant persons to the altar."

The Marquess of Alnwick was not the only one who wished to speak with the Prince of Wales. Captain Carswell had done so earlier and been told that he knew of no post currently open to the captain's particular talents. Especially not in view of certain events which had recently come to his ears, and just where were Major Langley and Captain Wollcott anyway?

Carswell had beat a hasty retreat, cursing himself for not forseeing the difficulties ahead. He also called at the Foster household and was told publicly not to post the notice of betrothal. The Fosters said, as an excuse to their friends, that Mary's family had to be privately informed before any formal announcement could be made. They could not bar the captain from calling, but it was made clear that under no circumstances would he be allowed to be alone with Mary.

As for Miss Farnham, more than one caller noted that her countenance could scarcely be called radiant and more than one person went away wagering upon the length of time the supposed betrothal would last. The Fosters, aside from expressing dire threats of what they would do to her if she dared to try to run away to go upon the stage, left Mary alone as much as was possible.

But Captain Carswell had more to worry about than a betrothal. It was noted that his friends, Langley and Wollcott, had left Brighton unexpectedly and that even the Viscount Halliwell appeared to be giving Carswell a wide berth. Indeed, the only encounter that could be vouched for between the two supposed friends occurred at the Foster household. Captain Carswell happened to be present when the viscount called to take his leave of the Foster family. To be sure, he greeted his friend amiably enough, but then it was noted that the viscount proceeded to entirely ignore the captain as he spoke to Miss Farnham and her aunt.

"I'm terribly sorry," Freddy said, taking hold of Mary's hand gently, "to have to leave Brighton while you are still here. Unfortunately, family business calls me to London and then my Yorkshire estate. May I hope to have the pleasure of seeing you again when I return?"

Interested eyes observed that Captain Carswell then rose to his feet, limped over to his friend and to his fiancée, clapped a hand on the viscount's shoulder, and said amiably, "Why Freddy, it appears you have not yet heard that Miss Farnham and I are to be married."

"I had heard, I simply had not believed it," Halliwell retorted with a grin. "When is the happy event to take place? Soon? Or have I time to return from Yorkshore first? I do want to be present."

Miss Farnham had colored prettily and Carswell had hesitated to reply, but Mrs. Foster had not. In her delightful voice she had said kindly, "Oh, it will be some time yet, Lord Halliwell. My husband and I mean to retire to our country home shortly and wish to have Mary with us for a little while longer. And of course she is still so young."

"Nineteen," Carswell said pointedly.

Gwendolyn Foster regarded the captain with raised eyebrows. "You know very well that in our family nineteen is considered a trifle young to be wed, whatever the custom may be in other households. After all, you have had to wait long enough as it is because of that."

Captain Carswell bowed and Lord Halliwell

beat a hasty retreat, with Carswell close upon his heels, hampered only by his cane. It did not go unnoticed that their conversation outside the Foster household was brief and that Carswell did not appear in the best of humor when he returned. Speculation could not help but grow as to why his friends were deserting him just then.

In some circles wagers were even taken as to when and if the formal announcement would appear.

Meanwhile, in London, a certain firm of solicitors was thrown into great distress by a number of events. The head of the firm addressed the more junior members in no uncertain terms. "We must locate Captain Carswell. Lord Atley's instructions were quite explicit in that regard and as to the measures we were to take to do so. He must be located as soon as possible and the matters at hand laid before him. He must be made aware of the stipulations Lord Atley has set forth if he does not wish to find himself penniless. None of you, or I for that matter, has met the captain. We are all, however, sufficiently cognizant of his reputation to realize that he is not likely to take kindly to Lord Atley's instructions. I believe we may anticipate a great deal of resistance to carrying out his lordship's requests. It is our duty to convince Captain Carswell that it is in his best interest to do so—that he cannot throw away what is otherwise offered to him. One of us must meet with him in person, once he has been located, to discuss precisely what is required and how he may best carry out the stipulations with the least distress to himself. The history of our firm's service to the Atley household requires that we do no less."

At the War Office, certain urgent discussions were being held concerning the disappearance of Major Langley and Captain Wollcott.

"They were to have reported here before returning to the Continent," one bureaucrat retorted irritably to the suggestion that the two military men had simply gone back to Wellington's staff. "And do you think they would have done so without Prinny's permission? I have it upon excellent authority that he knew nothing of their departure from Brighton. Nothing at all. There has been some sort of disaster, I tell you, some sort of disaster."

"Come, come, surely that is much too strong a word," another fellow protested.

"Not at all," the first bureaucrat said indignantly. "We all know what important papers Major Langley was carrying. And Captain Wollcott was to be his backup in case of trouble. If these papers have fallen into the wrong hands, well, gentlemen, I leave it to your imagination as to whether disaster is too strong a word or not!"

"Yes, yes," a third gentleman said soothingly, "but how are we to be sure?"

"Question Captain Carswell, perhaps? I understand he has been seen with them recently in Brighton," the second gentleman suggested hopefully. "After all, before he was invalided out Carswell was attached to the same company that they were and stood high on Wellington's personal staff. He may know something."

"Do you mean to suggest," the first fellow asked in appalled accents, "that Major Langley or

Captain Wollcott would have so far forgotten themselves as to mention such an important and such a secret mission to someone who no longer has any right to know about such matters?"

"Oh, do calm down," the third fellow said irritably. "I am sure that what Alfred meant is that having been a close friend of the major and the captain, Carswell may have spent some time with them in Brighton and be able to give us a clue as to why they left Brighton so suddenly and where they meant to go. Look, surely it's worth a try. What have we to lose?"

"Secrecy," the first fellow retorted bluntly. "One more person to know that we've lost track of two of our best men and some very important papers. For depend upon it, Carswell will be able to guess why we are so interested in the whereabouts of Major Langley and Captain Wollcott. And I cannot like such a breach of security as that."

The third gentleman took a deep breath to mask his exasperation and then asked patiently, "Yes, but what if he can tell us what we want to know?"

The first bureaucrat fixed his two companions with a long, level stare. After a moment he addressed the one who had spoken last. "If that is what you think, then you go and talk to Captain Carswell. But I warn you that if there is trouble because you have taken it upon yourself to do so, you will be held accountable for everything. I will not back you up."

"I never thought you would," was the audacious reply. Then, before the first fellow could say anything more, he bowed and added, "Well, I had best be going, hadn't I? The sooner I see Captain Carswell and talk with him, the sooner we may have an answer to our problem."

"No," the first gentleman said hastily. "At least give Langley and Wollcott until the first of the week to appear. If they haven't shown themselves by then, or we haven't received word as to their whereabouts, you may go to Brighton and see Captain Carswell. Is that clear?"

"Very," the younger man replied. He started for the door, then added maliciously, "In the meanwhile, why don't you try telling Prinny that he did see the papers and that he just forgot because he was under the weather at the time."

With a grin the fellow made a rapid retreat, entirely undistressed by the hearty oaths flung at his head as he did so. The important thing was that he would, in a few days, be on his way to Brighton and that he would be the one to interview Captain Carswell. And if there were problems, well, he would be the one to dispose of the matter. In whatever way was required.

21

PREPARATIONS were already in hand for the removal of the Foster household, including Mary Farnham, to the country when Hubert Foster burst into the breakfast room very late that Monday morning, newspaper in hand. His face was alarmingly red and he seemed almost incapable of speech as he threw the paper down onto the table in front of his wife and niece.

Gwendolyn Foster blinked in amazement at her usually peaceful spouse and asked, "Whatever is the matter, my love?"

Shaking a finger at his niece Hubert replied, "She is the matter, m'love. Or rather Captain Carswell is, which amounts almost to the same thing."

"It does?" Mary asked in astonishment.

"It does when the trouble is the formal notice, in the newspaper, of your betrothal to the fellow," Hubert confirmed. "This is, I suppose, another one of your absurd plans hatched out between the two of you. Well, by God, I won't have it! I'll send a retraction to the papers at once. And as for Captain Randall Carswell, he shall have to answer to me for this!"

* * *

The trouble was, Randall Carswell was using much the same words about Hubert Foster. "He was not to do this," he muttered aloud, pacing about his hotel rooms. "We were all agreed. So, Hubert Foster wants to see me wed to his niece. Well, by God, he shall answer to me for this one! I will not be forced into anything by anyone!"

The firm of solicitors in London had read the notice some hours earlier with unconcealed astonishment. "Can he be serious?" one of them asked.

"Perhaps he has already heard of Lord Atley's conditions," another suggested.

"Does it say where he is presently staying?" asked a third.

"Now that," observed the senior partner tartly, "is the first sensible comment I've heard yet. No, Mallory, it does not say where Captain Carswell is staying, but it does say that his fiancée is currently residing with her aunt and uncle in Brighton. I suggest you leave for there at once."

The bureaucrat from the War Office in London also read the notice quite early that morning. He found it mildly interesting, though he was not quite sure how it would affect his plans. He did decide, however, that he would no longer delay his journey to Brighton.

The Marquess of Alnwick, who was responsible for the uproar, did not even read the announcement, engrossed as he was in the pursuit of a provincial virgin in the west country.

* * *

The Viscount Halliwell, en route to Yorkshire, was handed a copy of the *Gazette* and almost turned around to go back. Then he consoled himself with the knowledge that whatever was afoot, no bride could be expected to find herself forced to the altar in less time than it takes to acquire the proper bride's clothes. And in his sisters' cases that had taken a good four months for each.

Two Frenchmen, Perrin and Dugard as they were known when they were in England, had not yet heard the news, but it would not have distressed them. They would have merely felt that it made the captain far more susceptible to blackmail.

At the estate of the late William Farnham near Stratford St. Mary, the notice in the *Gazette* produced even greater consternation than it had in Brighton. Gerald Kensley, Mary Farnham's stepfather, threw down the paper with an oath. "But my dear, whatever is the matter?" his petite blond wife asked helplessly.

"The matter?" Gerald Kensley said grimly, "is that your daughter has gotten herself betrothed."

"Well, but it had to happen sometime, I suppose," Mrs. Kensley pointed out diffidently.

"No it didn't," Kensley retorted. "Not if you'd looked after her as you ought to have and kept her home. Then if she had to take it into her head to marry, she might have decided to marry Thomas."

"But Thomas is her stepbrother," Mrs. Kensley objected.

"Well, what is that to say to the matter?" Mr.

Kensley demanded. "After all, it is not as though they were blood relations."

"But I don't think Mary particularly liked Thomas," Mrs. Kensley said thoughtfully. "At least I seem to recall her saying something of the sort."

"What has that to do with anything?" Kensley asked in exasperation. "A dutiful daughter would have married whomever you told her to."

"Me?" Mrs. Kensley asked with some surprise. "But I wouldn't have told her to marry Thomas. Think of the scandal. For there would be scandal, you know, even if they are not blood relations."

With exaggerated patience Mr. Kensley tried to explain matters to his wife. "The scandal from Mary marrying our Thomas, my dear, would have been nothing compared to the scandal that is going to occur if Mary actually marries this Captain Carswell."

"But why, dear?" Mrs. Kensley asked in bewilderment. "Is *he* a blood relation?"

"No, he is not a blood relation," Kensley replied with the same patience as before. "I don't know who the devil he is. But what I do know is that when your daughter marries I am going to have to turn over to her husband all the records concerning the trust your late husband left for her. And that is what is going to cause the scandal."

"Oh, dear," Mrs. Kensley replied. "What shall we do? Pay an extended visit to my cousins in Scotland?"

"If, my dear, I cannot succeed in preventing this wedding, I am not sure that even your cousins in South America will be far enough away," Kensley retorted with a roar.

As he rose from the table Mrs. Kensley called

after him, "Where are you going, my dear?"

Over his shoulder Mr. Kensley replied, not slowing his stride in the slightest, "To Brighton, dear wife, where else?"

Mary Farnham fled to her room and there hugged her pillow to her breast with a smile as she considered the awesome possibility that Captain Carswell did love her so well, after all, that he had defied her aunt and uncle and sent the notice to the *Gazette*. Lord Halliwell would no doubt have been quite startled were he to know that the thought of bride's clothes played no part in the delightful fantasies Mary Farnham spun in her head.

At the church in Ipswich a certain vicar read the notice with great satisfaction. "That will teach that young person, Miss Fane, not to believe in the promises of fickle gentlemen," he sniffed to himself over his morning tea. "Though I've no doubt that by now her downfall is so complete that she doesn't care in the slightest that her erstwhile gallant has become betrothed to someone else. No morals these modern girls have, none in the least! Someone ought to do something about it. I wonder if I ought to give a sermon about it this Sunday. Clarissa! More tea! In my study. I've a sermon to write."

Somewhere in England, two men were far too preoccupied with making secret arrangements to be ferried over to the Continent to bother with the notices in the London papers. After all, dealing with smugglers was a tricky business. And even if they had read the notice they would merely have assumed that an irate uncle had forced Carswell to the step and that that was one of the hazards, although admittedly a rare one, of war.

Thomas Kensley had heard about the notice in the *Gazette* from his father, but he really didn't care. He was far too interested, at the moment, in seducing a young girl from a nearby farmhouse. If, later, his father insisted he marry Mary Farnham, well, that was fine and good. The Farnham girl was terrified of him and would never expect him to spend much time in her bed.

Thomas was not entirely sure why his father was so eager for the match. He would have been surprised to discover that his family was not as rich as everyone, including Mary, had always believed. Gerald Kensley was not a man to confide in anyone.

Still, Thomas Kensley felt a certain anticipation at the notion of having a bride he could frighten. And he would greatly enjoy paying her back for the humiliation of discovering she had escaped him by running away. There was something indefinably exciting about the notion. But not enough to make him leave off his seduction of the farm girl to go to Brighton. Particularly when his capable father was willing to go instead.

Shelby was a rather curt little man. He resembled nothing so much as a minor tradesman, the sort of fellow the Quality would dismiss at a glance. His true profession, however, was closer to that of Bow Street Runner, and at the moment he was extremely interested in Captain Randall Carswell and his acquaintances. He read the notice with a grunt of something that might have been either approval or disapproval. In fact, it was indifference. As he had for the past two days, ever since Captain Carswell requested that he come down from London, Shelby had a neat little breakfast and then proceeded to unobtrusively shadow the captain everywhere he went.

It was rather late in the day when Captain Carswell and Hubert Foster encountered one another, roughly midway between the Fosters' Brighton residence and Carswell's hotel. Both had already been forced to endure the good wishes of more than one acquaintance who had seen the notice and neither was in the best of moods when they met.

"What the devil is the meaning of this!" they said practically in unison, each flourishing a copy of the *Gazette* at the other. "Why did you—"

They broke off in confusion as they realized what had just occurred. Suspiciously, Hubert Foster demanded, "Didn't you post this notice, Carswell?"

The captain shook his head. "No, I assumed that you had, highly irregular as such a step would have been."

"I?" Hubert said in surprise. "Why in God's name would I do that? I thought we were quite in agreement when you were at my house the other day. I was to pretend to have serious reservations about your marriage to my niece. That is why I was so astonished when I saw this notice. I simply assumed you were playing some new game. If I was wrong, I apologize."

"And I assumed you were trying to force my hand, although I must admit I could not understand why," Carswell replied grimly. "Who did send it then?"

"Frankly, I don't care," Hubert said, just as grimly as the captain. "What I care about is that this complicates matters greatly. I don't suppose you've had any luck in finding a means to support yourself?"

"I have written to my father telling him that I contemplate matrimony, and am waiting for his reply," Carswell said meekly. "I have some hope that he will see his way clear to increase the small allowance he has made for me. And I do have some savings left from when I sold out my captaincy."

Hubert Foster waved a hand irritably. "Yes, yes," he said, "but I meant something more reliable. Something with the War Office, perhaps?"

Once more the evils of Carswell's position came home to him. He shook his head and said, "Not as yet."

"Well, you've got to do something!" Hubert said in exasperation. "For your own sake, I just cannot imagine your hanging about doing nothing for the rest of your life. Have you no ambition at all? Nothing you would care to do?"

With a bitter smile Carswell replied, "Nothing practical or remotely possible."

"Well, what sort of impossible ambitions do you have?" Hubert asked, a trifle mollified. "Perhaps there is a way for you to do it."

Carswell shook his head again. "Not when both my brother and father stand in my way. I should like to have stood in the House of Lords and had a hand in deciding matters of importance to the nation."

"Why not stand for the House of Commons, then?" Foster demanded.

Quietly, Carswell replied, "Perhaps, if all else fails, I will. Meanwhile, however, what are we to do about this notice in the *Gazette*?"

Hubert Foster clapped a hand on the younger man's shoulder. "Oh, a pox on it! Let us go back to my house and try to discuss what to do. I've no doubt the ladies are already making wedding plans, but the same problems still exist. Perhaps if we put our heads together we can contrive something."

"I've a better idea," Carswell countered. "As you said, the ladies are probably hatching all sorts of wedding plans and that is not what we desire. Not at the moment, at any rate. Why don't we go back to my rooms instead."

Hubert Foster regarded the younger man with approval, and then laughed. "Capital notion, Carswell, capital notion. I knew there was something about you I liked. What a pity your circumstances present such difficulties. Otherwise, I should be quite pleased to have such a sensible nephew-in-law."

In remarkably good spirits, considering the circumstances, the two men started amiably together toward the Horn and Hare, the captain's limp as pronounced as ever.

22

WHEN Carswell and Hubert Foster reached the Captain's hotel they discovered that someone was waiting for him in the small lobby. The gentleman rose to his feet when he heard the clerk congratulate Captain Carswell on his forthcoming nuptials. The captain lingered a moment to thank the clerk and to speak to him about one or two trifling matters. The fellow in the lobby approached them. "Captain Carswell?" he said with a bow.

Carswell raised an eyebrow and looked over the stranger thoroughly. "Yes?" he asked politely.

"I need to speak with you," the fellow replied. "In private."

"I see. Concerning what matter?" Carswell asked in a most unencouraging voice.

The gentleman looked pointedly at Hubert Foster, who seemed as oblivious as Carswell to the hint, and then at the clerk, who hastily moved away to engross himself in other matters. Finally the stranger sighed in exasperation, then said, "Very well, concerning a matter of national security. To be precise, two members of

Wellington's staff need to be reached and we don't know where to find them. We have reason to believe you can help us."

"You'd best come up to my rooms," Carswell said curtly. "Foster, I am afraid we shall have to postpone our discussion until another time."

No one except Hubert Foster noticed the little man who had entered the Horn and Hare after Carswell and his guests and who now slipped quietly up the stairs.

"Of course," Foster said with a slight bow. "I shall see you later, Captain Carswell. Sir, your servant."

They watched Foster go and then Carswell, leaning heavily on his cane, indicated that the stranger should precede him to his rooms. When they reached the captain's private parlor and the door was shut behind them, Carswell nervously observed, "You have not yet told me your name, sir."

"You don't need to know my name," the stranger replied sternly. "What you do need to know is that we are trying to locate Major Langley and Captain Wollcott. We know they are friends of yours and hoped you might be able to tell us where to find them."

Carswell fiddled with a glass uncomfortably. "Would you care for a drink?" he asked the stranger. When the offer was declined he nevertheless poured himself one. Then, finally, he turned back to the stranger and said, a trifle too loudly, "I have not seen them since some time last week and I haven't the slightest notion where they may be."

"And yet you sent them a note to come and see you in Lullington," the stranger observed equally loudly.

Carswell visibly started. "How do you know about that?" he demanded.

The stranger waved a hand. "How I know is unimportant. The fact is that I do know. Now will you tell me what happened to them?"

Carswell shrugged and turned his back on the stranger. Irritably he replied, "How the devil should I know? Yes, I sent them a note suggesting they come visit me in Lullington, but they never arrived. They either never set out or else got sidetracked somewhere."

"And just what was so interesting about Lullington that you suggested they come see for themselves?" the stranger probed relentlessly.

"Look, just who the devil are you?" Carswell asked nervously.

"You do like that phrase, don't you?" the stranger observed mildly. Then, more loudly, menacingly, he added, "I already told you that I am with the War Office. But perhaps we can save ourselves a great deal of time if I also tell you that I know about Perrin and Dugard."

If it was at all possible, Carswell now went even more pale. The stranger went on, inexorably, "I know that you wrote, at their request, the note that was to bring Langley and Wollcott to Lullington. I know that you returned and they did not. I also know that two Frenchmen set off that night in a small boat out to a larger boat that then went straight to France." He paused then added, "I even know about the fire."

"What do you want of me," Carswell asked faintly.

"The truth," the stranger replied blandly. "Are Langley and Wollcott dead?"

"If you know everything else, then you know the answer to that as well," Carswell said roughly.

The stranger nodded, even though Carswell's back was still toward him. "Yes, I do know the answer," he said.

There was a long silence as he watched Carswell pace about the room. At last the captain said, again a trifle too loudly, "Does everyone in the War Office know about this?"

"No, only me. So far," the stranger replied, raising his voice to match Carswell's. "I thought," and again he paused before going on, "you might like to keep it that way."

Carswell spun around on his heel and stared at the stranger in disbelief. "You would do that for me?" he demanded eagerly. "Why? What do you want for your silence? Money? I haven't much nor any hope of raising more."

The stranger waved his hand carelessly. "There are other methods of payment, *if* one were to be so crude as to speak of such things, which we will not. Let us rather say that I am interested in acquiring your goodwill and your willingness to do me favors from time to time. Small things, or so they will seem to you, but of vast importance to me."

"I told Perrin I would not go so far as treason," Carswell said roughly.

"Who spoke of treason?" the other fellow asked. "Although one might say you had gone that far already." As Carswell's face darkened dangerously the fellow held up a hand and added quickly, "I do not say so, of course. I should rather lean to the notion that you are confused as to what is truly best for your countrymen. There are a great many men of considerable wisdom who ask why England should not make peace with Napoleon. You are merely one more of them and let us say your actions are toward making possible that end."

"You do agree, then, that the war should be ended at all costs?" Carswell asked eagerly, leaning toward the stranger. "You don't blame me for what I did?"

"Not at all, my dear fellow," the stranger replied. "In fact, I mean to help you do more for the cause in the days ahead. As someone with access to Prinny and other members of the *ton*, you could provide invaluable assistance to those of us working for peace with Napoleon."

"Not . . . not spying?" Carswell asked hesitantly.

The stranger laughed loudly. "My dear Captain Carswell, in my position at the War Office I can generally do all of that which is necessary. No, for the moment we have other plans for you, although we might, occasionally, ask for your assistance as we did with Major Langley and Captain Wollcott."

"So you were a part of that," Carswell said with a frown.

"Let us rather say I am kept well informed," the stranger countered. "Now, Captain Carswell, I need your answer. Will you assist us when called upon to do so?" Carswell hesitated and the stranger added menacingly, his voice rising as he spoke, "Or shall I have to regretfully inform the War Office of what I know of your involvement in the Langley/Wollcott affair? For they would believe me, you know, and any allegations you might make against me would be dismissed as the ravings of a man desperately trying to save himself from ruin. And I should not like to have to tell your fiancée's family what I know either. As you have pointed out, you are not precisely plump in the pocket, and I understand Miss Farnham is accounted something of an heiress. Surely, you would hate to have me destroy your plans in that direction?"

Carswell began to reply. "I—"

Before he could finish speaking the door to his hotel parlor crashed open and he and the stranger turned to find themselves confronted by a young lady holding a pistol gripped firmly in both hands.

"I suggest neither of you move," Mary Farnham said coolly, "or I should regretfully be forced to shoot you. Regretfully is the word you used, is it not, sir?" she asked, addressing the stranger.

Frowning Carswell demanded, "Mary! What the devil are you doing here and why do you have that pistol?"

Her voice may have trembled but her hands did not as Miss Farnham replied, "Uncle Hubert thought you might find your guest rather unwelcome, Captain Carswell. He told me enough that I could guess why. So I came prepared. In the hallway I listened at the door and heard enough to know that this man is threatening you, and I couldn't have that."

"You mean, judging by the timing of your entrance, my dear, that you couldn't have your precious captain answering me," the stranger suggested with a malicious smile.

"Th-that's not true," Mary retorted with a quaver in her voice.

"Then why did you say that neither of us should move or you would shoot?" Carswel asked, a hint of laughter in his voice. "Surely that is not a kind way to treat your fiancé?"

He took a step toward her and Mary raised her gun a trifle higher. "Very well," she said resolutely, "I was afraid to hear your answer. Because no matter how much I love you, I cannot allow you to betray our country." Her voice took on a note of desperation as she pleaded with him. "Don't you understand? They don't want peace, they want Napoleon to win. And they want you to help them. He says it won't be spying, but what was it when those Frenchmen managed to steal Major Langley's secret papers?"

His eyes round with astonishment, the stranger rose to his feet. "You know about those?" he demanded furiously.

"I—I—" Mary broke off in confusion as Carswell took a rapid step forward and wrested the gun from her hands.

In one smooth motion he seized her about the waist with his left hand, held the gun trained on the stranger with his right, and then said carelessly, "I keep no secrets from my fiancée, sir."

Mary tried to fight her way free, but Carswell paid no attention as she beat at his shoulders with her hands and said, "Let me go! Let me go right now!"

Instead, Carswell laughed again and then called loudly, "You can come out now, Shelby."

To everyone else's astonishment, a figure emerged from one of the cupboards. His erect carriage and unsmiling face made him seem taller than he was. Shelby nodded curtly to the captain, ignored Mary, and approached the stranger with a snort of contempt. "So Carswell was right," he said. "He told me someone in the War Office was working for Boney, but I didn't like to believe it. Not a pretty idea, is it?"

"What about him?" the stranger asked desperately. "He's the one who sold out his friends, Major Langley and Captain Wollcott. You must have heard him admit it?"

The fellow nodded. "I heard him. And that will

be taken under advisement. As will the fact that he's the one who suggested trapping you. Come along now. I've some superiors who will be very interested in talking with you. You can tell them anything you want about the captain's character."

As Shelby had drawn his own pistol and trained it on the stranger from London, the War Office bureaucrat made no resistance.

"Best be careful," Carswell suggested quietly. "He strikes me as a tricky fellow."

Shelby nodded curtly. "So he is. But I haven't lost a man yet and I don't mean to begin now. Well, come along. We've a bit of a ride ahead of us."

A few moments later they were gone and Carswell realized that although Mary had ceased to fight him, she stood trembling in his arms. With his free hand he set down her pistol and took hold of her chin instead. Tilting her face up to look at him Carswell asked, his eyes dancing with unspoken laughter, "Were you so very afraid for me, then? Or of me? What did you mean to do if I did betray myself as a traitor? And where in God's name did you get that pistol?"

Mary jerked her chin out of his hand. She would not meet his eyes as she said, "Uncle Hubert thought you might be in trouble. I knew where he kept a pistol in case footpads tried to break in at night. So I took it and brought it with me. Was I afraid for you? Yes. I knew that what you had done made you vulnerable to blackmail," she concluded defiantly.

Once more Carswell took her chin in his hand and this time did not let Mary pull free as he forced her to look up at him. "And what would you have done if I were a traitor?" he repeated insistently.

Mary's eyes filled with tears as she answered, her breath coming in ragged gasps, "I don't know. I meant to stop you, somehow, even if it meant kidnapping you and spiriting you away to the countryside somewhere. You're not really a traitor, are you? You've just been made so bitter by your injury that you can't think straight, can you? Surely you don't really want Napoleon to win?"

She broke off abruptly as she realized that he was laughing at her. "I don't see what's funny," she said in an aggrieved voice.

It was a few moments before Carswell could stop laughing sufficiently to reply, "You are delightful, my love!"

The captain kissed Mary on the nose and would have kissed her on the lips as well except that she drew her face away and said, in appalled accents, "Good God, you've gone mad, haven't you?"

Even this observation struck the captain as exquisitely amusing and he started laughing all over again. By which time his fiancée was looking even more distinctly unamused. Before he could say anything, however, there was another knock at the door and Hubert Foster entered, mopping his brow, followed by a young solicitor who bowed to the captain and said, "Lord Atley, may I offer you my felicitations on your forthcoming marriage?"

23

"**L**ORD Atley?" Carswell repeated blankly. "I think you've made a mistake. You must want my father."

A trifle testily the solicitor replied, "Yes, we do want your father. But as his death has made it impossible for us to serve his needs, I am here to tell you that my firm is ready to serve yours."

Carswell shook his head in disbelief. Then, in a careful voice, as though speaking to a madman, he said, "Now I don't believe, you understand, that my father is dead. But even if he were, it is my brother and not myself who would succeed to the title, surely. That is how an entailed estate works, isn't it? Surely you want my brother."

The solicitor closed his eyes as if in pain. After a moment he said patiently, "Yes, Captain Carswell, your brother is precisely the person we would want, if he were available. I have not dealt with either personally, but I am assured by other, more senior members of the firm, that both your father and brother are most amiable gentlemen."

"Well then," Carswell demanded, "what are you doing here? Surely you don't think to find them in Brighton?"

"No, I do not," the solicitor replied shortly, "for the very simple reason that they are both dead."

At last it seemed to penetrate to the captain that the solicitor was very serious in what he said. "I think you had better tell me what you mean," Carswell told the fellow quietly. Then, noting the man's parched look, he suggested, "Some wine, perhaps? You look as though you have had a fatiguing journey. You have come from London, I presume?"

"Yes, I have," the fellow agreed, looking somewhat mollified. "You are very kind. Perhaps a bit of brandy, if I might? My digestion is not what it ought to be when I must travel," he explained.

Carswell immediately poured the fellow a glass and showed him to a comfortable chair. He also provided a helping of brandy to Hubert Foster, who was watching the proceedings with grim interest. Somewhat dazed, Mary found a seat and declined Carswell's offer of something milder. Only when everyone was settled did the captain tell the solicitor to go on with his tale.

Nervously the solicitor gripped his glass as he explained. "I suppose you didn't know it, but shortly after you sold out your commission because of your injury, your elder brother secretly purchased colors for himself. Quite without your father's permission, I must add. But Lord Atley, when he discovered what your brother had done, made no effort to force him home. Instead, he instructed us that if that was your brother's choice, then he must live with it, and we were to discontinue his allowance until such a time as his lordship, the viscount, should cease to be a member of the military. I regret to say that the viscount was wounded in Spain a few weeks ago and died while returning back to England. He has already been buried at your home cemetery in Yorkshire."

"But if Charlie was that badly wounded, what was he doing traveling?" Carswell asked in bewilderment.

The solicitor coughed. "As to that, m'lord, I believe the wound itself was relatively minor and appeared to be healing nicely. There was, however, an infection that went unnoticed and carried him off before anyone realized how serious matters were. He was not the only one," the solicitor added after a brief pause.

"But my father," Carswell went on. "You said that he was dead as well."

"Your father had been ill for some time, although he chose to tell none of us," the solicitor said disapprovingly. "It was only when he called one of the members of our firm north for a final revision of his will that we realized just how ill he was. He felt, I believe, that he wanted to be a burden to no one. Nor could he abide deathbed scenes. Those are, I believe, the words he used to my colleague in the firm." The solicitor paused, then went on, "It is not my place to criticize your father, however had he been more forthcoming with his eldest son, I believe the viscount might not have chosen to purchase his colors and might still be alive today. But that is all beyond altering. The reason I am here today is to inform you, Captain Carswell, that you are now the Earl of Atley and to acquaint you with the stipulations laid down in your father's will."

The solicitor paused and looked around at Hubert Foster and Mary Farnham. To them he said, "Ordinarily I should feel that these provisions were a private matter and suggest that Lord Atley and I discuss them at a more convenient time. I collect, however, that you are Miss Farnham, the young lady mentioned in today's *Gazette* and therefore betrothed to Lord Atley. That is germane to the matter at hand. You, as her apparent guardian, Mr. Foster, may also find these provisions of concern."

He waited for them all to nod and Carswell found himself saying impatiently, "Well, go on with it. What conditions did my father set on me?"

The solicitor turned back to Carswell. "Well, you must understand that this will was made just after your father learned of your brother's death and realized that you would inherit the title." As an aside he added, "I've no doubt that the shock of your brother's death hastened his own end. By the time my colleague reached your father's estate, Lord Atley was already quite weak."

"The provisions," Carswell prompted through gritted teeth.

"Oh, yes, the provisions of the will. Well, m'lord, you won't find the first one too cumbersome because it requires that you marry within six months. The second is that should your wife have cause to complain of your treatment toward her, the estate is to be placed in the hands of trustees who will administer it for her and her offspring until you die and the next Lord Atley inherits. You would have the title but little else. That also holds true if you were to refuse to marry."

The solicitor coughed and corrected himself, "Well, you do not have to marry within six months but that is the grace period given you. After that, if you are not married you have little but the title, a situation that alters immediately should you marry at any later point in the future though the second provision still holds true. Is that quite clear?"

"Quite clear," Carswell confirmed from between still gritted teeth. "Did my father have any other delightful stipulations concerning me?"

Nervously the solicitor nodded. "Oh, my, yes. Though they primiarily have to do with care of the tenants on your land. You are expected, however, to spend at least six months a year on your estates looking into their care and condition. Also, our firm is required to approve your choice of bride. But there will be no difficulty in this case as Miss Farnham is evidently a most unexceptionable young lady. That is the primary requirement."

"That she be unexceptionable?" Hubert Foster spoke for the first time.

"No, no, that she be a lady," the solicitor replied. "The late Lord Atley was afraid, you see, that Captain Carswell might, er, well, choose someone of unsuitable status. An, er, actress or something."

A sort of choked gasp came from Mary and the solicitor addressed her anxiously. "Oh, my dear young lady, you need have no fear," he said earnestly, "that someone could mistake you for a member of the demimonde. No, no, your breeding is quite acceptable to the firm. We took the liberty of looking into your parentage this morning and already you have been approved by no less than the senior member of the firm himself."

Mary merely held her handkerchief closer to her face and nodded. Somewhat impatiently Carswell asked, "Well, any other conditions? Come, you may as well tell me the worst."

A trifle waspishly the solicitor replied, "I have

already said there are none you need worry about, m'lord. You are evidently not addicted to drink and close to ruin from that source. And if you have persuaded a family as respectable as the Farnhams to welcome you into their midst, you have evidently not taken up a life of professional gambling or taken to the roads as a highwayman, nor are you wallowing in a life of depravity." He paused, then said with some asperity, "I must say, the late Lord Atley did have quite an imagination. Having met you, m'lord, I cannot conceive what possessed him to put such questions into his will!"

"Thank you," Carswell said gravely. "May I ask what my next step is?"

"Yes," the solicitor said, rising to his feet. "We should like you to come to London, if that is not too much trouble, and sign certain documents. We can then acquaint you with all of the provisions in greater detail. Oh, and of course we will look for your wedding within the six-month stipulated period. If that is agreeable to you, I will leave you with your fiancée and her guardian and arrange for a room for myself for the night. If you have any further questions, I shall of course be available."

He took his leave of them and when he was gone, Mary, Foster, and Carswell looked at one another in astonishment. Hubert was the first to speak. He clapped his hands on his knees and said, blinking rapidly, "Well, I must say this does change things. When I said you ought to alter your prospects, Carswell, I mean Lord Atley, I had nothing so drastic as this in mind."

Amused, Carswell asked, "I collect, then, that you now have no objection to my marriage to your niece?"

"Having just spoken with Shelby," Hubert

replied, "I have none at all, providing Mary has none."

Looking at Miss Farnham, Carswell said, "Perhaps you ought to leave us alone so that I can ask her."

"Leave you alone?" Foster asked, startled. "Most improper! Even if you are engaged. And that reminds me, Mary. If I had had any notion that you would be so foolish as to come here, alone, just because Captain Carswell had an unwelcome visitor, I would never have told you."

"Yes, but she thought I might need rescuing," Carswell replied for her. Foster regarded the captain sharply but he looked innocently back at the man and, after a moment, suggested, "Perhaps you could just step outside the door or into my bedroom, then. No one would know you had left us alone."

"Impossible," Hubert started to say grimly.

Carswell forestalled him by rising to his feet, his cane once more forgotten, and holding out an imperious hand to Miss Farnham. "Come, Mary," he said amiably. "Your uncle is perfectly right. I should never have asked him to go into the bedroom. You and I shall go in there."

Mopping his brow feverishly, Hubert was at once on his feet. "No!" he cried. "That is, I shall be happy to go outside the door for a few minutes. But only a few minutes, mind you. And I hope to God you set an early date for the wedding. I really cannot imagine myself chaperoning the pair of you for much longer!"

When he was gone Mary looked at Captain Carswell and quickly looked away, drawing in her breath as she did so. He was staring at her with grim determination and now he possessed himself of both her hands. "Well, Mary?" he asked her.

"Will you marry me, now that I have sunk myself beneath reproach and become Lord Atley?"

Stung, she looked up at him and said sharply, "You are roasting me! You know very well I should never have looked to marry an earl and it is a change in your position that can only make you more acceptable to anyone."

"But I'm not interested in anyone," he said meekly. "I'm interested in you and how you feel. Will you marry me, Mary?"

With a wrench Mary pulled her hands free and turned away from him. "I wish I could," she said over her shoulder. "But what about your friends, Langley and Wollcott?"

"They won't mind," Carswell assured her.

"That is not what I meant!" Mary retorted in exasperation. "I meant, what about what you did, helping Perrin and Dugard get those papers? Do you think I could marry a man who had betrayed his country? No matter how much I thought I loved him?"

Delighted, Carswell took a step toward her. "Do you love me, then?" he asked.

Not trusting herself to speak, Mary nodded. With a cry of triumph, Carswell put his arms around her and drew her onto his lap as he sat quickly in the nearest chair. Mary tried to pull free but without success. When she finally gave up trying, and felt herself close to tears, Carswell began to kiss her gently. First on her eyelids, then on her nose, finally on her lips. Of their own accord it seemed, Mary's arms wrapped themselves around the new Lord Atley's neck. When he was satisfied she wouldn't try to escape anymore, Carswell lifted his lips from hers and looked down into her eyes.

"I'm not a traitor, you know," he said softly.

"Perrin and Dugard were meant to get those papers. It was Langley's idea and he asked me to help him. Those papers contain false plans meant to mislead Napoleon into a possibly fatal error. But I couldn't tell you, or anyone. And that man today? We've been trying to catch him for some time. We knew there was a traitor in the War Office, but we didn't know who he was. Our game with Perrin and Dugard was meant to flush him out as well. Even your uncle helped by pretending to disapprove of me. And it worked." As Mary stared at him in wide-eyed astonishment, Carswell kissed her again. Then he said, his eyes twinkling, "You, or rather Jeremy, were a most unexpected, worrisome quirk in the plan. I was terrified they would hurt you somehow."

"And I was so afraid they would hurt you," Mary countered.

Carswell's grip tightened around her and he asked fiercely, "You do mean to marry me, don't you?"

"Before or after the six months are up?" Mary asked innocently.

"I don't give a damn whether it's before or after the six-month limit," he growled at her, "except that I warn you, I'm likely to grow extremely impatient if you try to make me wait that long!"

Meditatively, Mary looked at him and said, in a languishing voice, "That's true. And after all I needn't fear that you will be the sort of husband who tries to beat me or ride roughshod over me, for if you do I can always tell the solicitors and have them tie up your inheritance."

Her look was a challenge and Carswell met it. He kissed her again, quite thoroughly, and when he was done, said softly in her ear, "I shall be the best husband I know how to be. But if you ever again do anything as outrageous as you have done in the past few days, I'll take you over my knee and the inheritance be damned. Although," he added in a meditative voice of his own, "I rather think that in that case the solicitors might take my side anyway."

As he was about to kiss her once more Hubert Foster entered the room without knocking. "There you go again," he said. "Behaving outrageously just as though I wasn't anywhere nearby. Precisely the reason I didn't want to leave you two alone. The wedding is settled, I presume? It had better be, otherwise I just don't know what I'm going to do with the pair of you."

"The wedding is settled," Carswell agreed gravely. "At least between Mary and myself. The formal marriage agreements will need to be drawn up, but the solicitors can handle that."

Hubert mopped his brow again. "Well, good," he said grudgingly. "That's all right and tight, then." A thought suddenly occurred to Foster and he said, a trifle anxiously, "Except, that is, for Gerald Kensley. He is her guardian and he won't like this. He won't like this at all. I shouldn't be surprised if he comes straight to Brighton the moment he reads the notice in the papers."

The new Lord Atley rose to his feet, gently setting Mary on hers as he did so. "Let Kensley come," he said grimly. "I wish him joy of what he will find to be a fruitless trip."

"What will you tell him?" Mary asked.

Carswell looked down at her reassuringly. "I shall tell him that you are going to marry me. And that if he tries to object he will find himself up before the law on charges of stealing your inheritance."

"Stealing my inheritance?" Mary asked blankly.

"I told you you weren't to tell her," Foster said annoyedly.

Carswell regarded them both implacably. "Why not? Mary has no illusions about her stepfather and she may as well know the extent of the damage he has done her. You are not precisely penniless, Mary, but I should guess Kensley has gambled most of it away. As I shall point out to the blackguard, if you marry me, no one need ever know."

"I don't like the idea of his getting off scot free," Foster said with a shake of his head.

Putting his arms around Mary again, Carswell replied, "Neither do I, but I find that at the moment very little seems important compared with the knowledge that I'm soon going to marry a woman I am very much in love with."

Mary reached up a hand to stroke his cheek, causing Foster to snort again in disgust. "Very pretty behavior. Right in front of me and neither of you has sufficient sense of shame to restrain yourselves! What the deuce do you expect me to do?"

"Go home and wait for Mary's stepfather to arrive, at which point you can explain the facts of the situation to him," Carswell replied without looking at Hubert, who growled warningly. With a sigh the new earl looked away from Mary and said, "Oh yes, I suppose you ought to take her with you. Mary, I shall come to call early tomorrow and we shall make all our plans then."

"Are we really going to be married?" Mary asked, smiling up at him. "It still seems a little unreal."

"Yes, we really are going to be married," the new Lord Atley reassured her. Then, after a pause, he added, "So long as no one tells the solicitors, anyway, that my bride-to-be once planned to tread upon the stage!"

About the Author

April Lynn Kihlstrom was born in Buffalo, New York, and graduated from Cornell University with an M.S. in Operations Research. She, her husband, and their two children enjoy traveling and have lived in Paris, Honolulu, Georgia, and New Jersey. When not writing, April Lynn Kihlstrom enjoys needlework and devotes her time to handicapped children.

COMING IN MARCH 1988

Sandra Heath
A Matter of Duty

Marion Chesney
The Savage Marquess

Gayle Buck
Lord John's Lady

SIGNET REGENCY ROMANCE

A Signet Super Regency Romance

"Spectacular, sensual, scintillating interplay
between two heartwarming lovers . . . a winner!"
—*Romantic Times*

INDIGO MOON

by Patricia Rice

bestselling author of *Love Betrayed*

*Passion ruled her in the arms
of a Lord no lady should love
and no woman could resist*

*Lady Aubree Berford was a beautiful young innocent,
who was not likely to become the latest conquest of
the infamous Earl of Heathmont, the most notorious
rake in the realm. But as his bride in what was
supposed to be a marriage-in-name-only, Aubree must
struggle to stop him from violating his pledge not to
touch her . . . and even harder to keep herself from
wanting him. . . .*

A Signet Super Regency

"A tender and sensitive love story . . . an
exciting blend of romance and history"
—*Romantic Times*

The Guarded Heart
Barbara Hazard

Passion and danger embraced her—
but one man intoxicated her flesh
with love's irresistable promise . . .

Beautiful Erica Stone found her husband mysteriously mur-
dered in Vienna and herself alone and helpless in this city
of romance . . . until the handsome, cynical Owen Kings-
ley, Duke of Graves, promised her protection if she would
spy for England among the licentious lords of Europe.
Aside from the danger and intrigue, Erica found herself
wrestling with her passion, for the tantalizingly reserved
Duke, when their first achingly tender kiss sparked a
desire in her more powerfully exciting than her hesitant
heart had ever felt before. . . .

There's an epidemic with 27 million victims. And no visible symptoms.

It's an epidemic of people who can't read.

Believe it or not, 27 million Americans are functionally illiterate, about one adult in five.

The solution to this problem is you... when you join the fight against illiteracy. So call the Coalition for Literacy at toll-free **1-800-228-8813** and volunteer.

Volunteer Against Illiteracy. The only degree you need is a degree of caring.